"I'd like to see you again," Ryder began.

Lynn watched his gaze fall to her lips. He stood so close that she could see gold flecks in his dark irises. "I'm flattered, Ryder, but no."

"No?" he echoed.

How could she go out with Ryder? When Gary had been alive, the three of them had been the best of friends. She thought of Ryder as a—a brother-in-law. "I don't think it would be a good idea for us to form that kind of friendship. There are too many ghosts."

His eyes narrowed. Then he reached out and gently touched the side of her face.

Warmth radiated from his light caress, and intense sensations assaulted her. She lowered her gaze, searching for an explanation for what was happening to her. A brother-in-law shouldn't make her feel like this. A lover, maybe, but not a brother-in-law....

DEBBIE MACOMBER

For All My Tomorrows

MIRA BOOKS

ISBN 1-55166-156-X

FOR ALL MY TOMORROWS

Printed in U.S.A.

To Aunt Nancy
and Uncle Joe Zimmerman—
my mother's favorite brother,
Arizona's favorite comedian
and
my kind of hero.

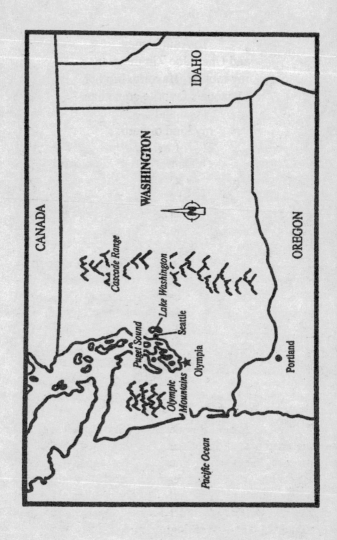

Prologue

The mournful sound of taps cut through the coarse gray afternoon. Lynn Danfort stood tall and proud before her husband's casket, refusing to release the emotion that viciously clawed at her chest. Her two children were gathered close at her sides, as though she could hold on to them tightly enough to protect them from the reality of this day.

Seattle's police chief, Daniel Carmichael, assisted by Ryder Matthews, neatly folded the American flag that rested atop the polished casket and calmly presented it to Lynn. She tried to thank the police chief, but realized she couldn't speak. Even nodding was more of an effort than she could make.

When they'd finished, Pastor Teed spoke a few solemn words, and then slowly, in coordinated movements, Gary Danfort was lowered to his final resting place.

Lynn repressed a shudder as the first shovelful of dirt slammed against his casket. The sound reverberated in her ears, magnified a thousand times until she yearned to cover her head and scream out for them to stop. This was her husband...the father of her children...her best friend...and Gary Danfort deserved so much more than a cold blanket of Washington mud.

Shot in the line of duty. Pronounced dead at the scene of the crime. At first Lynn had refused to believe her husband was gone.

The thick dirt fell again, and Lynn believed.

The tightening in her chest worked its way up the constricting muscles of her throat and escaped on a sob as the shovel was handed in turn to the men and women who had so proudly served with Gary. The trembling increased as each dull thump echoed like a somber edict in her tortured mind.

Hope was gone.

Dreams destroyed.

Death the victor.

Tears welled like boiling liquid in the corners of her eyes, her first for that day. She'd wanted to be strong—it was what Gary would have wanted—but now she let them fall. The moisture seared crooked paths down her ashen cheeks.

A voice violated her pain. "It's time to go."

"No."

"This way, Mrs. Danfort."

Again she shook her head. "Please. Not yet."

Her strength was depleted, and for the first time since she'd learned of Gary's death, she needed someone—someone she loved, someone who had loved Gary. She looked around for Ryder. Her friend. Gary's partner. Godfather to their children.

Her gaze scanned the crowd until she found him, standing in front of Chief Carmichael.

A protest swelled in her throat as she watched him pull his badge from his wallet and place it in the police chief's palm.

Ryder turned to her then, his pain and grief as strong as her own. She could see that Chief Carmichael was trying to reason with him, but Ryder wasn't listening. His gaze reached over the crowd of mourners until it found Lynn. Their eyes met and locked.

Lynn pleaded with him not to leave her.

His gaze told her he must. Regret clouded the harsh features as his eyes shifted to Michelle and Jason, her children.

Then, silently, Ryder Matthews turned and walked away.

One

"Lynn, there's a call for you on line one."

"Thanks." She reached for her phone and pressed it against her shoulder, securing it with her ear. "Slender, Too, this is Lynn speaking."

"Mom?"

Lynn released a silent groan and rolled her eyes toward the ceiling. It wasn't even noon and this was the fifth phone call she'd received from the kids. "What is it, Michelle?"

"Jason ate the entire box of Cap'n Crunch cereal. I thought you'd want to know so you could take appropriate action."

"I didn't take it all." Jason's eight-year-old voice echoed from the upstairs extension. "Michelle ate some, too."

"I didn't."

"Did, too."

"Didn't."

"Michelle! Jason! I've got a business to run!"

"But he did, Mom, I swear it. I found the empty box stuffed in the bottom of the garbage. And we all know who put it there, so don't try to lie your way out of this one, Jason Danfort. And, Mom, while I've got you on the phone, I think you should have a serious discussion with Jason about his Rambo Club."

Lynn closed her eyes and prayed for patience. "Michelle, this conversation will have to wait until I'm through here. Where's Janice?"

It was the third week of June. School had been out for a grand total of five days, and already Michelle and Jason were at each other's throats. The high-school girl, whom Lynn was paying top dollar to baby-sit the kids, had revealed all the maturity of an eleven-year-old, which was Michelle's age. One child responsible for two more. This wasn't working, and Lynn's options were limited.

"Janice is checking the garbage to see what else Jason's hiding in there."

"Mom, you can't expect me to live like this," her son interjected. "A man is a man. And a man's got to do what a man's got to do."

"Right," Lynn responded without thinking.

"You're agreeing with him?" Michelle's shrill voice echoed her outrage. "Mom, your son is stealing food and you seem to think it's perfectly all right."

"I'm going out on a mission," Jason cried in self-defense. "I could be gone three or four hours doing surveillance. I'll need nourishment, but if you're so concerned about your stupid cereal, I'll put it back."

"Can you put a hold on this war until I get home?" Lynn demanded of the two.

Silence.

Lynn mentally calculated a list of effective threats that had worked in the past. Regrettably her mind came up blank. She was a strong, effective businesswoman, but when it came to her children she was at a loss as to how to deal with them—especially in matters such as stolen Cap'n Crunch cereal.

"Lynn." Sharon Fremont, her assistant, stuck her head around the door. "Your aerobics class is ready and waiting."

"Listen, kids, I've got to go. *Please* don't fight and don't call me at work unless it's an emergency."

"But, Mom . . ."

"Mom!"

"I can't talk now—I've got a class waiting." Lynn checked her watch. "I'll be home by four. Now be good!"

"All right," Michelle muttered. "But I don't like it."

"Me, either. If I'm not home when you get here," Jason whispered into the phone, "you know where to find me."

"You think you're so smart, Jason Danfort," Michelle whined, "but I know your hiding place—I have for weeks."

"No, you don't."

"Yes, I do."

"*Kids*, please!"

"Sorry, Mom."

"Yeah, sorry, Mom."

Lynn replaced the phone. Michelle and Jason claimed they were sorry. Somehow she doubted that.

The house was suspiciously quiet when Lynn let herself in at three-forty-five that same afternoon.

"Michelle?"

Silence.

"Jason?"

More silence.

"Janice?"

"Oh, hi, Mrs. Danfort."

The fifteen-year-old appeared as if by magic, and every aspect of her peaches-and-cream complexion spelled guilt. The teenager rubbed her palms back and forth and presented a forced smile.

"Where are Michelle and Jason?" Lynn asked, and slipped the sweatband off her forehead. She hadn't taken time to shower, preferring to hurry home dressed in her turquoise spandex leotards and top, in an effort to deter yet another world war.

"They're both gone," Janice announced, her eyes avoiding Lynn's. "That's all right, isn't it?"

"It's fine."

"Oh, good."

Lynn reached for the mail, shuffling through the pile of bills and setting them back down on the counter unopened.

"Jason's with his Rambo friends, and Michelle's over at Stephie's listening to some rap tapes."

"That's fine. I'll see you tomorrow morning then."

"Sure," Janice said and was through the door before Lynn could figure out why she wore the look of a cat burglar caught with a bagful of goodies.

Mulling it over, Lynn traipsed over to the fridge and took out a cold soda—her pop-for-the-day. This was a family rule—no one drank more than one can a day, otherwise they would go through a 12-pack by noon.

She sat, plopped her feet on the chair across the table from her and took a sip, letting the cool liquid revive her.

"Mom," Michelle called, as she raced through the front door. She stopped abruptly when she found Lynn in the kitchen.

"Hi, sweetie," Lynn answered and smiled. "Did you ever solve the Cap'n Crunch caper?"

"Jason pulverized it into sand and poured the entire bag into his canteen." She raised her eyes toward the ceiling in mute testimony to what she thought about her brother's odd ways. "You've got to do something about him, Mother. That cereal was half mine, too, you know."

"I know... I'll talk to him."

"You say that, and then nothing ever happens. He should be punished. That boy has no sense, and you're not helping. He honestly thinks he's another Rambo. Any other mother would put a stop to it."

"Michelle, please, I'm doing the best I can. Wait until you're a mother...there are just some things you have to make judgment calls on." Lynn couldn't believe she'd said that. It was like an echo from the past, when she'd battled with her younger brother and her mother had said those identical words to her.

"At least let me decide Jason's punishment," Michelle cried. "I know that boy better than anyone. Let me give him what he deserves."

"Michelle..."

"Mom." The screen door burst open and Jason roared into the kitchen, dressed like Rambo, his mock machine gun raised high. He let loose with a scream that threatened to crack the walls and then fired imaginary bullets toward the ceiling.

Michelle plugged her ears and cast her mother a look that spoke volumes.

"Jason, please," Lynn pleaded, placing her fingertips to her temple. "If you're going to fire your gun, do it outside."

"Okay," he answered with a grin, and cheerfully lowered his weapon.

Her son was dressed in his camouflage pants and a grimy green sweatshirt. His face was smeared with green coloring and a thick black stripe was painted under each eye. His knees were caked with mud, and he looked as if he'd battled long and hard all afternoon.

"So how's the war going?"

"We won."

"Naturally," Michelle said in a know-it-all voice that caused Jason to slowly turn in her direction, raising his gun as he did so.

"Not in the house," Lynn reminded him.

"Right," he answered slowly, baring his teeth at his sister.

Michelle placed her hand over her flat chest. "I'm shaking in my boots with pure terror at the thought of you coming to get me."

Jason's eyes narrowed into menacing slits. "You better do something about her, Mom, or she's going to suffer a slow, painful death."

"Jason, I don't like you talking like that."

"Answer me this," he cried with indignation. "Does Sylvester Stallone have to put up with a big sister like this one?"

"You're not Sylvester Stallone."

"Not yet," he said forcefully. "But someday I'm going to be."

Lynn prayed this was a stage her son was going through because, like Michelle, she'd about had it with Jason's war machine.

"When are we leaving for the picnic?" Michelle asked, glancing toward the bulletin board.

"Picnic?" Lynn echoed. "What picnic?"

"The one Dad's ol' police buddies invited us to—the one with the notice on the bulletin board."

Lynn dropped her feet and whirled around to check her calendar. "Is today the twentieth?"

Both Michelle and Jason nodded.

"Oh, great," Lynn muttered. "I'm supposed to bring potato salad."

"Do what you always do," Jason suggested. "Buy it at the deli. Why should today be any different?"

Lynn reached for her drink and hurried toward the stairs, taking them two at a time. She stripped off her top and reached blindly toward the shower dial when she noted the bathroom counter. Something stopped her, but she didn't know what. Something wasn't quite right.

In a flash, she recognized what was different. Reaching for a towel to cover her torso, she stormed out of the bedroom. "Michelle. Jason. Front and center— pronto."

Both kids came racing into her bedroom.

"All right," she said, her voice wobbling, "which one of you got into my makeup?" Her gaze narrowed, and what she saw on her son's face answered her own question. "Jason...that's my green eye shadow all over your face! My *expensive* green eye shadow."

"Mom, your shower's running," Jason said, pointing in that direction. "You're wasting precious liquid, and you always say how we should conserve water. Remember the drought a couple of years ago—you wouldn't want to start another one, would you?"

"He used my eye shadow," Lynn announced to her daughter, while she returned to the bathroom to turn off the shower. The day had started off badly. First Michelle and Jason had found every excuse known to mankind to call her at the office, and now this!

"If you look real close, you'll note the black under his eyes looks a lot like something you wear on *your* eyes, too," Michelle said once Lynn reentered the room.

"My eyeliner, too?"

A look of betrayal crossed Jason's young features. "Okay, Michelle, you asked for this. I wasn't going to tell, but now you're forcing my hand."

Michelle stiffened. "You wouldn't dare," she whispered.

Jason squared his shoulders. "Michelle and Janice were in your room this morning, Mom. I felt it was my duty to find out what they were doing—"

"Jason..." Michelle's frail voice rose an octave, pleading.

"They were trying on your bras. The real fancy lace ones."

"Oh, my God." Lynn sank onto the foot of her bed. Nothing was sacred anymore. Not her makeup. Not her underwear. Nothing. And worse, she was paying a teenage neighbor girl top wages to snoop through her drawers.

"Mom," Michelle moaned. "I need a real bra...you haven't seemed to notice, but I'm filling out my training one." She paused and turned to face her traitor brother. "Get out of here, Jason. This is woman talk."

"Trust me, Mom, she doesn't need anything. She's as flat as—"

"Jason!" Lynn and Michelle cried simultaneously.

He jerked up both hands. "All right, all right. I'm out of here. I felt you needed to know the truth...I was only doing my duty as your son and as Michelle's brother."

Lynn's fingers were trembling as she ran them through her thick brown hair. She reached behind her head and released the clip that held her hair neatly in place.

"You and Janice aren't allowed in my bedroom, young lady," she said. "You know that."

Michelle buried her chin in her shoulder blade, looking miserable.

"I can't have you sorting through my things while I'm at work."

"I know...I'm sorry," Michelle murmured, still not looking at her mother. "We didn't mean to try them on, but they looked so pretty and Janice said you'd never know, and I didn't think it would hurt until Jason—"

"This just isn't working," Lynn whispered. "You and Jason are constantly bickering. Janice is fifteen, going on ten. I can't stop running my business just because you kids are out of school. It may be summer, but we still have to eat!"

"It won't happen again," Michelle promised. "I'm really sorry."

"I know, honey." But that didn't change things. Janice was too immature to be watching Michelle and Jason, and the children were too young to stay on their own.

Michelle straightened her shoulders. "What are you going to do to Jason for getting into your makeup? I know I shouldn't have tried on your bras, but Jason shouldn't have gotten into your things, either."

"I don't know yet," Lynn answered.

"Hey, are we going to the picnic or not?" Jason demanded from the other side of the bedroom door.

"He was listening," Michelle whispered with righteous indignation. "I bet you anything, he had his ear to the door and the minute we started talking about him, he broke in."

"We're going to be late for the picnic if you two don't stop this," Lynn commented, eager to change the subject.

She hated to think what Michelle and Jason would do once they learned she was putting them in a day-care center. They were going to hate it, but she couldn't help that.

After what had happened today, her mind was made up.

Two

Toting the toy machine gun in one hand, and with a blanket tucked under the other, Jason marched across the park lawn with crisp military precision. With his head held high and proud, he angled toward the assigned picnic area at Green Lake. Lynn and Michelle, holding the handles of the picnic basket between them, followed.

Lynn's smile was forced as she raised a hand to greet the men and women who had once worked with her husband. She remained good friends with several of the other wives on the force, although there were lots of new faces these days.

"I'm so pleased you could make it," Toni Morris called out, walking toward Lynn. "It's good to see you, stranger!"

Lynn let go of the basket and hugged her dear friend, who was a former policewoman. She didn't see nearly enough of Toni these days and treasured the few times they could be together. "It's good to be here."

"How's everything?"

Lynn knew that pert and practical Toni would easily see through a false smile and a cheerful facade. This summer had gotten off to a rotten start, and she was troubled. With the other police wives, she could grin and nod and claim her life was a bed of rose petals and because they wanted to believe that, they wouldn't question her.

But not Toni, who had married an officer of the law herself and who was well aware of life on both sides of the coin.

"Life's so-so," Lynn answered honestly. Afternoons like this one made her feel she had failed as a mother. Like so many other women, she wore two hats—one for work and another at home. Michelle and Jason came first in her life, but she *had* to earn a living. What Slender, Too, didn't drain from her energy tank, the kids did. She felt stretched to her limits, and there was only so much elastic in her.

Toni slipped her arm around Lynn's waist, glanced in Michelle's direction and pointed toward a picnic table with a red checked cloth spread across the top. "Michelle, go ahead and set your stuff next to mine. Kelly's getting her feet wet at the lake. Go on down and surprise her—she's dying to see you."

"Oh, good! Wait until she sees my hair, she's going to flip," Michelle announced, and raced like a speeding bullet, taking the basket with her.

"Okay," Toni murmured, looking thoughtful. "Tell me what's wrong?"

For lack of a more precise answer, Lynn shrugged. "Nothing's working out this summer the way I hoped it would. Michelle and Jason are constantly bickering. The baby-sitter is snooping through my drawers. Jason's into this Rambo stage and is slowly driving me bananas. He doesn't seem to make the connection between what happened to Gary and that toy machine gun he totes."

"He doesn't," Toni assured her. "He's a perfectly normal eight-year-old, and this thing with the Stallone

war games is just a stage he's going through. Both
Michelle and Jason are perfectly normal kids."

"I don't know if they'll ever get used to me working.
I swear they use every excuse in the book to phone me
at work. Michelle wanted me to know Jason used the
ink up in my felt-tip pen. And Jason was convinced
Michelle hid his plastic army knife from him. And then
there was a fiasco over the Cap'n Crunch cereal. Honestly, Toni, how can I be expected to supervise them and
run a business, too?"

Toni's look was sympathetic.

"It's as if they feel the need to compete for my attention," Lynn added. "I don't know what to do anymore."

"Who's watching them this summer?"

"A neighbor girl, and I think that's a major part of
the problem. Michelle's at that transitional age when
she's too young to stay by herself and yet resentful of
having someone baby-sit her. I'd hoped to solve that by
hiring a neighborhood girl, but it simply isn't working."

"Can you find someone else?"

Lynn shrugged again. "At this late date? I doubt it.
And the programs at the 'Y' filled up so fast it made my
head spin. Parents register months in advance for summer day care."

Toni studied her a moment longer. "It's more than
problems with the kids and summer vacation, though,
isn't it?"

Lynn had to stop and think about that. Toni was
right—she usually was. For the past several months
Lynn had been experiencing a restlessness that came
from the deepest part of her inner self. She hadn't been

sleeping well and often awoke feeling depressed and out of sorts, without understanding why.

"You're not taking care of yourself," Toni said, after a thoughtful moment.

Lynn blinked, not sure she understood her friend. She'd never been more physically fit—in fact she looked as good, if not better, than she had as a twenty-year-old bride. Her hair needed to be cut, but finding the time was the biggest hangup there.

"You can't always be the perfect mother *and* the astute businesswoman," Toni went on to say. "You need time to be you."

"Me?" Lynn repeated. She wasn't exactly sure who *she* was anymore. There'd been a time when her role in life had been clearly defined, but not anymore. Since Gary had died, she viewed herself as a quick-change artist who leaped through hoops—some small, others large—in an effort to make it to the end of the day or the end of the week. She felt as if she'd been cast adrift in a lifeboat and she was the only one strong enough to man the oars.

"Be good to yourself," Toni continued. "Splurge. Take a whole day and relax at the beach or shop to your heart's content."

"Good idea," Lynn whispered, feeling a nearly overwhelming urge to cry. "I'll do exactly that the next time I find the time."

"When did you last go out on a date?"

"I haven't in months, but don't try to convince me that's the problem," Lynn said, her voice sharp and strong. "It's a jungle out there, with lots of lions and tigers roaming about. After my last hot date with a forty-year-old mechanic who lives with his mother, I decided I'd let Mr. Right find me. I'm done with the dating scene. Finished. Kaput.''

"The mechanic was a tiger?" Toni gave her a look that suggested therapy was sure to help.

Lynn sighed. "Not exactly. He was more of a warthog."

"And exactly what type of beast interests you? A cheetah? Gorilla?"

"Tarzan interests me," Lynn said, and laughed. Soon Toni's chuckles mingled with her own.

"Come on now, Lynn, you're not really serious about refusing to date anymore? You're too young to resign yourself to life alone."

"I'm not interested in remarrying—at least not for now." There'd been a time, albeit short, when Lynn had seriously considered finding another husband and making a new life for the kids and herself. She hadn't expected Prince Charming to come charging into her living room atop a white stallion, but she hadn't been prepared for all the court jesters, either. Soon after she'd reentered the dating world, she'd discovered how shockingly naive she was and exited with a speed that convinced her friends she hadn't tried nearly hard enough. Her friends, however, were married or involved in satisfying relationships. They weren't the ones forced to mingle with warthogs and court jesters.

"There's something you should know," Toni announced, tossing a glance over her shoulder.

"Don't tell me you've got someone here you want me to meet. Toni, please, don't do that to me."

"No, not that."

"What, then?"

"Someone's here all right, but I didn't bring him."

"Who?" Her friend had seldom looked more serious. Lynn had been aware the entire time they were talking how Toni had kept her on the outskirts of the group. Sensing that whatever her friend had to say was important, Lynn met her look, feeling Toni's anxiety.

"Ryder Matthews stopped by," Toni announced. "In fact, he's here now."

"Ryder," Lynn echoed, her voice little more than a hoarse whisper. Emotion circled her like smoke rising from a camp fire, twirling around her, choking off a reply. Lynn wasn't exactly sure what she felt. Relief mostly, she decided, but that was quickly followed by resentment that flared, then vanished as fast as it came. Ryder had turned his back and walked away from her— literally and figuratively. A week after Gary's funeral a letter with a Boston postmark had arrived from Ryder. He'd told her he'd had to go away, and asked her forgiveness for leaving her and the kids when they needed him most. He promised her that if she were ever to need anything, all she had to do was let him know and he would be there. Lynn didn't doubt his word, but she never asked—and Ryder had never come. He promised to keep in touch, and true to his word, he'd faithfully remembered Michelle and Jason on their birthdays and Christmas, but he never directly wrote Lynn again.

And now Ryder was back. Ryder Matthews. She loved him like a brother, but she couldn't help resenting the way he'd abandoned her. She didn't want to have anything to do with him, but she'd needed him at one time and then had gone about proving exactly the opposite. Her thoughts were as knotted and twisted as pine wood.

"Are you going to be all right?" Toni asked.

"Sure. Why shouldn't I be?" But she wasn't. Lynn felt as though the entire world had been briefly knocked off its axis. She squared her shoulders and stiffened her spine, mentally and physically preparing for whatever was to follow. She'd waited a long time to talk to Ryder and now she hadn't a clue about what she was going to say.

"Apparently he just moved back to Seattle," Toni added.

Lynn nodded, not knowing how else to respond.

"He's an attorney now and recently joined some prestigious uptown law firm. He kept in touch with several of the guys, but his return surprised everyone."

Lynn knew that Ryder had been accepted into law school following graduation from college but had grown restless after the first year, eager to make a more concrete contribution to society. After he dropped out, he'd applied and was accepted into the police academy, where he'd met Gary.

"Well," Toni urged her. "Say something."

"What's there to say?"

"I don't know," Toni admitted. "But every time Joe's talked to him the last couple of years, all he does is ask about you and the kids."

"Wh-what did he want to know?"

"How you were. How the kids were doing. That sort of thing. He may have stayed away from you, but I know for a fact that you were never far from his thoughts."

"He could have asked me himself."

"Yes, he could have," Toni agreed. "I'm sure he's going to want to later. I just felt you should know he's here so it won't come as a shock."

"I appreciate that," Lynn said, although she wasn't sure there was anything to say to Ryder. There had been once, but not now.

Ryder Matthews spotted Jason first. Gary and Lynn's son had sprouted like a weed, and just catching a glimpse of the boy produced an involuntary smile. He looked like a miniature Sylvester Stallone, dressed in fatigues with a green sweatband strapped across his forehead as though he planned to stalk through a jungle at any minute.

Ryder's gaze left the youth to scan the picnic area. He located Michelle next. The preteen was standing by the lake, talking to another girl. She'd changed, too. The girlish features had disappeared, and the promise of a special beauty shone from her sweet oval face. Her hair was shorter now, the pigtails and bright ribbons replaced with carefully styled curls. The eleven-year-old was several inches taller, too, as was Jason. Ryder smiled, pleased with the changes he noticed in them both.

A couple of minutes later, he allowed his gaze to search for Lynn. Gary's Lynn... *his* Lynn. When he found her, talking to Toni Morris in the picnic area, a rush of air left his lungs as though someone had playfully punched him in the stomach. She was everything he remembered and more. God only knew how he'd managed to stay away from her so long. He'd never forgotten her face, or the athletic grace with which she moved. The sunlight had always seemed to bounce off her hair, and the only way he could think to describe the husky sound of her voice was smoky molasses. He recognized every line of her creamy smooth face, which was dominated by high cheekbones, a stubborn chin and that wide, soft mouth.

Lynn's hair was much longer now, the thick dark length woven in a single French braid that gently fell against her back. She wore fashionable white shorts and a pink tank top that showed off her golden tan. She carried herself with such pride and grace that it humbled him just studying her. Ryder watched as she smiled and waved to another friend, while standing with Toni. She paused and glanced in his direction. Although Ryder was fairly certain she hadn't seen him, he felt the physical impact of her smile halfway across the park. He'd always found Lynn attractive, had admired her from the first, but the years had matured her elegant beauty.

Just looking at her caused his heart to swell with pride. Everything he'd learned about her revealed an inner fortitude. She was strong, stronger than he'd realized. She'd walked through the valley in the shadow of grief and destruction and come out the other side, confident and strong.

Ryder loved her for it.

The need to talk to her burned in his chest. There was so much that had to be said, so much he needed to explain. It had taken him three long years to surface from the tragedy of Gary's death. Three years to come to grips with himself.

For the first one, he'd submerged himself in his classes, preferring to bury his head in books and study until all hours of the night. Anything but sleep, because sleep brought with it the nightmare he longed to forget. Law school had given him a purpose and an excuse. There wasn't time to think, and for the next twelve months school anesthetized him from the pain.

The second year had been much the same, until the anniversary of Gary's death had arrived. He hadn't been able to sleep that night, playing back the details in his mind over and over again until his heart had started pounding so violently he could hardly breathe. He knew then that he would have to deal with the emotions surrounding his partner's death, or they would haunt him for the rest of his life unless he sought professional help. That second year had been the most draining; it had been the time he'd dealt with his feelings for Gary and, perhaps even more importantly, his feelings for Lynn.

It happened unexpectedly, when he was the least prepared to deal with it, following a conversation with Joe Morris, Toni's husband. Joe had told Ryder that Lynn had started to date a mutual friend, Alex Morrissey. At first, Ryder was pleased because he longed for Lynn to find a new life, but he wasn't thrilled with her choice of men. Lynn could do better than Alex. He was relieved when he called Joe a few weeks later and found out that Lynn had stopped seeing Alex but had accepted a date with Burt, another mutual friend. But Ryder didn't like Burt any better—he was downright irritated about the whole matter. Burt would make a terrible stepfather and Alex wouldn't be much better. In fact, Ryder couldn't think of a single man worthy of Lynn and Michelle and Jason.

Then it came to him so sharply that he was left stunned by the shock. He was in love with Lynn and had been for years. When Gary was alive, the three of them had been inseparable—the very best of friends. He hadn't realized his feelings for her then, hadn't been honest enough with himself to have been able to face it.

It had been an old joke between them, the way Ryder had drifted in and out of relationships. Little wonder! Every woman he ever dated simply couldn't compare to Lynn. He may have been close to acknowledging what was happening, because he'd started thinking about returning to law school long before Gary's death. But after the tragedy, his love for Lynn had been so repressed it had taken two years for him to even recognize his feelings for her.

Knowing what he did, the third and final year of law school had been sheer hell. Ryder's greatest fear was that Lynn would find someone to love and remarry before he could get back to her.

Now he was back, ready to build bridges with the past, ready to start life all over again. Everything hinged on Lynn. Not a day went by that he didn't think about her and the children. Not a night passed that he didn't plan their reunion.

For the first time in years, Ryder felt a strong urge to reach for a cigarette. Years of habit directed his hand to his empty shirt pocket. A momentary sense of surprise was followed by a chagrined pat against his chest. He'd given up the habit before joining the force, and that had been a lifetime ago. How odd that he would feel the need for a smoke now, after all these years.

"Toni," Lynn asked without looking up from the table where Michelle had set their picnic basket. "Have you seen Jason? He disappeared the minute we arrived." She sliced a pickle in half and added it to the pile on the plate. "Knowing him, he's probably doing surveillance, checking out the area for enemy agents." She paused and licked the juice from her fingertip, and reached for another dill pickle. It was then that she realized she was talking to thin air. Toni was standing across the picnic area from her.

"Has he found any yet?"

The strong male voice froze her fingers, and slowly Lynn raised her eyes to meet Ryder Matthews. "Found any?" she asked, hardly able to speak. Just seeing him again brought a throb of excitement.

"Enemy agents?" Ryder asked.

She shook her head. The weight of his gaze held her prisoner. Instinct told her to go back to the task at hand, act nonchalant, friendly. "Hello, Ryder," she managed finally when her heart had righted itself. "It's good to see you."

"Hello, Lynn." His voice was warm and husky. It felt like a warm blanket wrapped around her shoulders on a cold winter night.

"Toni mentioned that she saw you earlier," she said, taking pains to keep her voice even.

"I thought she might have." He stepped closer to the picnic table.

"Want a pickle?" It seemed crazy that she hadn't seen Ryder in three years and all she could think to do was offer him something to eat.

"No, thanks."

Her fingers trembled slightly and she slipped the knife through the cucumber and added the slices to the plate. "She also said she'd heard something about you passing the bar."

"She heard right."

"Then congratulations are in order." Once more she struggled to keep her voice and emotions on an even keel.

"Lynn..." He paused and rubbed the back of his neck as if weighing his words. "It's time we talked," he said slowly, thoughtfully.

The silence that followed screamed at her. She expelled her breath and dropped her hands to the table. "That isn't really necessary. I know why you're here."

Three

"**Y**ou know why I'm here?" Ryder echoed, his frown darkening.

Lynn closed her eyes and nodded. She'd known almost immediately why Ryder had left her alone the day of the funeral. She also knew why he'd found it essential to resign from the police force. Seeing him confirmed it. Even the most casual study of his features revealed that the years had weighed heavily upon him. Although they were close to the same age, Ryder looked several years older. She'd forgotten how tall he was—well over six feet, with wide shoulders and a powerful torso. His hair was as dark as his eyes, and his features had a vividness that drew her gaze to his face as effectively as a puppet's string. A soft smile touched the edges of her mouth as she pictured him standing in front of the jury box delivering the final argument to an important case. She was pleased with the image that formed in her mind. Ryder would do well as an attorney, but then Ryder Matthews was the type of man who would succeed at whatever he set out to accomplish.

When Toni had announced Ryder was at the picnic, Lynn's feelings had been ambivalent. Her instinct had been to lash out at him, hurt him the same way he'd hurt her, but she realized now how senseless and immature such thoughts were. She couldn't do that. Ryder had suffered, too, perhaps even more than she had. He hadn't left her because he'd wanted to—he'd gone because the pain had been too overwhelming to allow him to stay. Law school had just been a convenient excuse.

"Probably more important," Lynn told him, smiling sadly, her heart aching for them both, "I know why you went away."

"Lynn, listen—"

"Please, this isn't necessary." Her long nails pressed against the underside of the picnic table as she leaned her weight against it. "You've blamed yourself, haven't you? All these years you've carried the guilt of what happened to Gary."

Ryder didn't answer her, but pain flashed in and out of his eyes like a flickering light until he regained control.

"Don't. Gary loved his job. It was his life—what he was meant to do. He knew the risks, accepted them, thrived on them. I knew them, too." She had to keep talking, had to say what needed to be said before she succumbed to the emotion welling inside her throat and choked off her voice. Ryder had lived with the regrets and the guilt long enough; it was time for her to release him so he could make peace with himself. It was the reason he'd come to her, and she could do nothing less for the man she'd once considered family.

Ryder looked away and then slowly shook his head. "I was the one who told him to walk around the back of that house. It was my decision, my choice, I—"

"You couldn't have known," she said, cutting him off. "No one possibly could have guessed. It wasn't your fault—it wasn't anyone's fault. It happened. I'm sorry, you're sorry. The entire Seattle Police Department is sorry, but that isn't going to bring Gary back.''

Time had done little to erase the memory of the tragic incident that had led up to her husband's death. Everything had been so routine, so mundane. Gary and Ryder had been called to investigate the report of a suspected prowler. The two men had arrived on the scene and split up. Ryder went to the left, Gary to the right. A crazed drug addict, desperate for another fix, had been waiting. He panicked when Gary stumbled upon him, and frantic, the addict had turned and quickly discharged his weapon. A wild shot had gone through Gary's head, killing him instantly.

"It should have been me." Ryder's words were harsh and ground out, each one a breathless rasp from his lips.

"No," she countered. "I can't blame you, and I know in my heart that if Gary were standing here right now, he wouldn't fault you, either."

"But—"

"How he loved working with you." Her voice cracked and she bit into her lower lip until she'd composed herself enough to continue. "The best years he had on the force were the ones spent as your partner. The two of you were more than fellow officers, you were friends. Good friends. Gary loved his job because you were such a big part of it."

Ryder lowered himself onto the bench beside the picnic table, leaned forward to brace his elbows against his knees and clasped his hands. "He trusted me, and I let him down."

"You trusted him, too. It wasn't you who fired that gun. It wasn't you who turned on him. Fate did, and it's time you accepted that. I have. There's no bitterness left in me. I couldn't go on—couldn't even be a good mother, if my life were marked with resentments.''

Ryder was silent for so long that Lynn wondered what he was thinking. His brow was creased in a weary frown, his eyes dark and unreadable. He held himself so completely still that she feared he'd stopped breathing.

''We should have had this discussion long before now,'' he murmured.

''Yes, we should have,'' Lynn returned. ''But you've corrected that. You're free now, Ryder, truly free. Nothing's going to hold you back any longer—your whole life is about to start again. It's your time to soar.''

Slowly he rose to his feet, his frown intact. He studied her closely, as though he didn't know how to respond to her.

''I wish you the best, Ryder. You're going to do well as an attorney. I know it—I can feel it in my blood.'' She felt the urge to hug him but suppressed it. Instead she made busywork around the picnic table. ''It really was good to see you again.'' She could feel the weight of his eyes on her, demanding that she look at him.

''I'm back now,'' he said. ''I intend to stay.''

''I...heard that. I'm happy for you and proud of everything you've managed to accomplish.'' She lifted the container of potato salad out of the picnic basket and set it in the middle of the table.

''I'd like to see you again.''

Lynn fiddled with the paper napkins. ''I suppose that will be inevitable. The precinct tries to include the children and me in their social functions. We attend when we can. I imagine you'll receive the same invitations.''

''I didn't mean that way. I want to take you to dinner, spend time getting reacquainted...date.''

Lynn's gaze, which she'd so carefully trained on the checkered tablecloth, shot upward. She was sure she'd heard him incorrectly. Was Ryder talking about a date? It would be like having dinner with her own brother. He couldn't have surprised her more had he suggested they climb a tree and pound their chests like apes. She opened her mouth, then closed it again when no fleeting words of wisdom surfaced to rescue her. In addition to everything else, Lynn was well aware of Ryder's dating habits. He never went out with any woman for long. It used to be a big joke between her and Gary how Ryder used to drift from one relationship to another. The longest she could ever remember him dating one woman was a couple of months.

"I'd like to gain back that closeness we once shared," he elaborated.

"We already know each other, in some ways probably better than we know ourselves."

"And there are ways we haven't even begun to explore."

Lynn watched as his gaze gently fell to her lips. They stood so close that she could see gold flecks in his dark irises. Doubt and pain mingled there with another emotion she couldn't identify. The desire to ease his pain welled inside her. She longed to wrap her arms around him and absorb the hurt and let him soak up hers. Once more she resisted, attributing these strange feelings to the closeness they'd once shared.

"Well?" he asked, though not impatiently. "Can I pick you up tomorrow night for dinner?"

She shook her head. "I'm flattered, Ryder, but no."

"No?" he echoed, surprised.

"I could give you any number of reasons, but the truth of the matter is I simply don't have much time for a social life right now. I bought a business, and the kids keep me hopping, and frankly, I don't think it would be a good idea for us to form that kind of friendship—there are too many ghosts.''

"Because of Gary?" he asked. "Or is it because I walked away from you?"

"Yes...no...oh, heavens, I don't know." She glanced at her watch and was shocked to see that her hand was trembling. "I have to round up the kids now, so if you'll excuse me."

His eyes narrowed, and Lynn could see that he was debating on whether or not he should argue with her. Apparently he'd decided against it, and Lynn was grateful. Instead he reached out and gently touched the side of her face. A warmth radiated from his light caress, and Lynn blinked, having difficulty sorting through the sensations that assaulted her. Her stomach muscles constricted, and her heart shot into her throat. A brother shouldn't make her feel this way. A lover maybe, but not a brother. Something was wrong with her, terribly wrong.

"I want you to think about it." He dropped his hand and removed a business card from his wallet. "Give me a call when you change your mind...or if you need anything. I'm here for you now."

Lynn picked up the card and read his name and phone number, searching the words as though they could reveal what was happening to her.

"I mean it, Lynn."

For the past year, Ryder had planned this first meeting with Lynn, going over and over it in his mind, practicing what he was going to say until he'd memorized each line, each bit of dialogue. Yet nothing had gone as he'd planned, nothing had happened the way he'd hoped. Lynn had assumed he'd been crippled by guilt and that was what had kept him away all these years. Until she started to speak, Ryder hadn't realized how many unresolved feelings he still harbored for his late partner.

Everything had been so clear in his own mind. He knew what he wanted and knew what he had to do in order to get it. It shouldn't come as any big surprise that it wasn't going to be easy to escape the ghosts from the past. But then, Ryder realized, obtaining anything of value rarely came without effort.

He was so deep in thought that he didn't notice the boy who stood in front of him until the lad spoke. The dark brown eyes studying Ryder were wide and serious.

"You're Uncle Ryder, aren't you?"

Ryder was astonished, Jason was hardly old enough to remember him.

"My mom has a picture of you and my dad on the fireplace," Jason explained, before Ryder could question him. "You send me something for my birthday every year and Christmas, too. You buy real good gifts. I wanted to send you a list last year, but mom wouldn't let me."

Grinning, Ryder asked, "So you recognized me from my picture?"

Jason nodded. "Except you've got a different color of hair on the side of your head now."

Ryder smiled at that. "I'm getting old."

"You used to be my dad's best friend, didn't you?"

"We were partners."

"Mom told me that, too." Jason paused and removed a canteen from his belt loop. With a good deal of ceremony, the eight-year-old opened the lid and poured a granulated pink-and-wheat-colored substance into the palm of his hand. When he'd finished, he lifted the canteen to Ryder in silent invitation. Without knowing what it was that Jason was eating, Ryder held out his open palm. When Jason had finished, Ryder sampled the mixture and decided that whatever it was, it didn't taste bad.

"It's cereal," Jason explained. He was silent for a moment, frowned and then asked, "Do you have any older sisters?"

"One."

"Yeah, me, too. They can be a real pain, can't they?"

"At times." Ryder finished licking up the last of the crumbs, then brushed his hands free of the granules. "But trust me, Jason, girls have a way of improving with age."

"That's what my grandpa says, but personally I can't see it. Rambo doesn't have anything to do with them, except to save their lives."

"Your dad saved mine once."

Jason's eyes brightened. "My dad saved your life? Really?"

Ryder nodded, regretting bringing up the subject of Gary, but it was too late now. "More than once actually."

"Can you tell me about my dad? Mom talks about him and you a lot—or at least she used to before she bought Slender, Too. She told me she doesn't want me to forget him, but to tell you the truth, I hardly remember anything about him, even when I try real hard. My mom talks to me about the mushy things he used to do, like getting her roses on their anniversary, but she never talks about the good stuff."

Now that he'd fallen into the trap there wasn't anything to do but continue. Jason was hungry for information about his father, and it would be unfair to cheat the boy. "Gary Danfort was a special kind of man."

"Tell me about how he saved your life."

"Sure," Ryder answered and chuckled, then he talked nonstop for thirty minutes, relaying story after story about his exploits with Gary Danfort. They both laughed a couple of times and Ryder was surprised by how good he felt. In fact, he'd never missed Gary more than he did that minute, talking to the other man's eight-year-old son. Ryder expected the kind of raw emotional pain that came when he thought of his former partner, but instead he experienced a cleansing of sorts that would have been difficult to put into words.

When he'd finished, Jason's wide brows knit together, forming a ledge over his deep brown eyes. He looked as if his eager mind had soaked in every word, like a dry sponge sipping up spilled water.

"Mom told me he was a hero," Jason commented, when Ryder had finished, "but I never knew exactly what he did."

"You're going to be just like him someday," Ryder told the youth, and was rewarded with the widest grin he'd ever seen.

"The man who killed my dad's in prison," Jason added, unexpectedly, "but Mom said I should try not to hate him because the only person that would end up hurting is me."

Ryder wished he could be as generous in spirit. "Your mother is a wise woman."

"She's hardly home anymore the way she used to be," Jason added, and released an elongated sigh. "She bought a business last year and it takes up all her time.

She's only home afternoons and nights now, and when she is, she's pooped."

Ryder frowned. He remembered when he'd heard about Lynn buying the franchise, and thought it would be good for her. "What does she do there?" He assumed she'd taken over the management, but not an actual teaching position.

"She makes fat ladies skinny."

"I see." Once more Ryder was forced to swallow a chuckle. "And how does she manage that?"

Jason pointed a finger at the sky and vigorously shook it three times. "Exercise. Exercise. Exercise."

Unable to hold it inside any longer, Ryder laughed aloud.

"It's not really funny," Jason said. "These ladies are serious and so is Mom."

"It's not that, son."

Faintly, in the distance, Ryder heard Lynn calling Jason's name. The youngster perked up immediately. "I've got to go. I bet it's time to eat. Are you going to sit with us? Mom forgot all about the picnic until Michelle reminded her. We were supposed to bring potato salad, but Mom picked some up at the deli. It's not as good as what she usually makes, but it tastes okay. We brought along hot dogs and mustard and pickles my Grandma put up last summer and a bunch of other stuff, too. You don't have to worry about not bringing any food because we've got plenty. You can stay, can't you?"

Four

"I don't like this one bit," Jason muttered from the back seat of the five-year-old Honda Civic.

"To be honest, I'm not overly pleased myself," Lynn returned, tightening her grip on the steering wheel. Jason was so outraged at the prospect of spending his summer with a bunch of preschoolers that he'd refused to be in the front seat with her. But where her son chose to sit was the least of Lynn's worries.

"I'm too old to be in a day-care center."

"You're too young to stay by yourself."

"Then how come Michelle gets to stay with the Morrises?"

"We've been over this a hundred times, Jason. Michelle is staying with Mrs. Morris until I can find someplace permanent for her."

"What's the matter with Janice? She may be a little ditzy, but she was all right."

"How many times do I have to remind you that I can't trust the three of you alone together? You know why as well as I do."

"But, Mom, I can handle Janice."

"That's the problem!"

"Why can't I stay with Brad?"

"His mom works, too."

"But why can't I go where he goes?"

"I tried to get you into the day camp, but it's full. Your name's on a waiting list, and as soon as there's an opening you can switch over there."

"I can't believe you're doing this to me," Jason muttered disparagingly. He crossed his arms over his chest and sulked.

"Jason, I'm your mother. Trust me, I don't like it any better than you, but there doesn't seem to be any other solution. Maybe later in the summer a better idea will present itself, but for now, you're going to the Peter Pan Day-care Center."

"The Peter Pan Day-care Center?" Jason cried and bounced his head against the back of the seat. "I suppose you want me to call the teacher Tinker Bell."

"Don't be cute."

"If Dad were here, this wouldn't be happening."

Jason might as well have punched her in the stomach; his words had the same effect. The pain rippled out from her abdomen, each circle growing wider and more encompassing until the ache reached her heart and centered its strength there. Since Jason had met Ryder, he'd used every opportunity to bring up his father—and Ryder. But using Gary against her was unfair.

"Well your father *isn't* here," Lynn returned sternly, "and I've got to do what I think is best."

"Putting me in with a bunch of little kids is the best thing for me?" Jason cried, his voice filled with righteous indignation. "I'm not a baby anymore, Mom."

"Third grade isn't exactly high school."

"I can't believe my own mother is doing this to me," her son grumbled, sounding as though she'd turned traitor on him and was selling him into a life of slavery.

"Will you stop laying on the guilt," Lynn cried. "I feel bad enough as it is."

"If you felt that bad, you'd find a place with a different name. I bet Sylvester Stallone's mother would never have done anything like this to him."

"Jason!"

"Peter Pan, Mom?"

"Think positive . . . you could teach the other boys your war games."

"Right," he said, but his voice lacked any enthusiasm.

After Lynn had left a tight-mouthed Jason at the day-care center, she drove to her salon. This last week hadn't been her best. If matters had been shaky before the precinct picnic, they were worse now. One of her instructors had quit, leaving Lynn to fill in until a replacement could be hired and trained. The night before she hadn't gotten home until after six and both kids were tired, hungry and cranky—an unpleasant combination. If that wasn't bad enough, Jason had been bringing up Ryder's name every afternoon like clockwork until Lynn was thoroughly sick of hearing about the man. She had trouble enough dismissing Ryder from her mind without Jason constantly talking about him. He repeated word for word what Ryder had told him about his father and the reason Ryder couldn't stay and eat with them the day of the picnic.

Lynn was smart enough to realize that it wasn't Jason's chatter that disturbed her. It was the fact that her son mentioned Ryder's name in such a reverent whisper, as though he were speaking of Rambo himself. Lynn's feelings toward Ryder were still so muddled and unclear, she wasn't sure she could identify them. Even if she could, there wasn't time to do anything about them. What had really confused her was his dinner invitation. It had been more than a surprise—it had been a shock. As much of a jolt as seeing him again had been. She felt girlish and immature and uncertain of everything. After Gary's death, she'd faltered for a while, and staggered under the weight of shock and pain. It had taken her a long while to root herself once more, and find purpose for her and the children. But those few minutes with Ryder had knocked her off balance more than anything else since Gary's funeral.

The only thing they had in common anymore was their love for Gary. Ryder may have suggested getting together for dinner, but Lynn was convinced it had been a token offer. He was probably as surprised at himself for even suggesting it. He hadn't contacted her since, and she was grateful.

By noon, the same day she'd dropped Jason off at Peter Pan's, Lynn was exhausted. She was working at her desk, nibbling her lunch, when her assistant stuck her head in the door.

"A Mr. Matthews is here to see you. Should I send him in?"

The pen Lynn was holding slipped from her fingers and rolled across the desktop. She caught it just before it fell off the edge and onto the floor.

"Mr. Matthews?"

"Yes," Gloria answered, and wiggled her eyebrows expressively. "He's cute, too. Real cute. He's got a voice so husky it could pull a sled."

"Ah..." Lynn tried to laugh at her employee's joke while glancing frantically around the room, seeking an excuse, any excuse, to send Ryder away. None presented itself. It was one thing to talk to Ryder at Green Lake where there were blue skies and lots of people. But it was another matter entirely to sit across her desk from him, when she was wearing pink leotards and a sleeveless lavender top.

"Lynn, what about Mr. Matthews?"

"Sure, go ahead and send him in."

"A wise decision," Gloria whispered, and pushed open the door so Ryder could step inside.

He walked into her tiny office, and his presence seemed to stretch out and fill every corner and crevice in the room.

Lynn stood, her heart pounding as fast and hard as a piston in a clogged engine. "Hello, Ryder. What can I do for you?" She hoped her voice sounded more confident than she felt.

"Hello, Lynn. I've got the afternoon free and since I was in the neighborhood, I thought I'd stop and see if you could have lunch with me."

This second invitation surprised her as much as his first one had. She twisted around and pointed to her unopened yogurt and a rye crisp that was only half gone. "As you can see, I've already eaten."

"That doesn't look like much of a lunch to me."

"I wouldn't dare bring a hamburger in here," she said, forcing a smile. "I'd be mobbed."

Ryder chuckled and pulled out a chair.

Reluctantly, Lynn sat, too.

"I hadn't heard from you." He spoke first, looking strong and confident. His mouth twisted into a slow, sensual smile that told her he'd been waiting for her.

A simple smile caused her stomach to knot.

"I was hoping you'd call," he added.

Lynn blinked, wondering if she was missing something. "I was supposed to contact you?"

Ryder nodded. "You were going to consider going out to dinner with me."

Lynn's eyes widened involuntarily. "No, as I remember, I said I didn't have the time and that I felt it was better for us to leave matters between us the way they were."

"I asked you to dinner; I didn't suggest an affair."

Extending her lower lip, Lynn released a breath that was strong enough to ruffle her bangs. "Ryder... you've been gone three years. You were Gary's best friend; you were *my* friend, too, but my life is different now."

"So different you can't indulge in one evening's entertainment?"

"Yes... I mean, no." Even now Lynn wasn't exactly sure why she felt she had to refuse his offer. Something elemental, a protective device she'd acquired since becoming a widow, slid securely into place. "I can't," she answered after a brief hesitation, her voice strong and determined.

"Why not?"

"Ryder, this is crazy. I'm not anything like the women you used to date. I think of you as a friend and a brother... not that way."

"I see."

It was obvious from the way he was looking at her that he didn't. "But more importantly," she felt obliged to add, "you don't owe me this."

"*Owe* you this?" The smile vanished, replaced with a piercing dark gaze that would intimidate the strongest personality.

"It's been three years now, and you seem to feel—"

"You amaze me the way you assume you know what I'm thinking," he said and stood, bracing his hands against the edge of the desk. "This time you're wrong."

His face was only a few inches from hers, and, although she tried not to look at him, his gaze dragged hers back to his. She braced herself, for *what* she didn't know—a clash of wills, she supposed. Instead she found herself sinking into the control and power she found in his eyes. It was like innocently walking into quicksand. It demanded all her strength to pull herself free. She was so weak when she managed to look away that she was trembling.

"Will you or won't you go to lunch with me?" Ryder asked.

He could have been asking about the weather for the casual way in which he spoke, but Lynn noted his voice had acquired a different quality. And yet his words weren't heavy or deep or sharp. She blinked, not sure what was happening to her or if her mind was playing games with her. What she saw and heard in Ryder was *purpose*. He wanted something from her and he wasn't about to give up until he achieved it.

"I . . ."

"Lunch with an old friend isn't so much to ask."

Lynn braced herself and kept her tone as even as possible, belying the jittery, unstable feeling inside her. "Ryder...I have my own life now. I just don't have the time to dig up the past, and, unfortunately, all we have in common anymore is Gary."

He said nothing, and his silence was more profound than the most heated argument. Lynn knew Ryder, knew him well, or at least she had at one time. He was intelligent and perceptive, and she prayed he could make sense of her jumbled thoughts even if she couldn't.

"I'll give you more time—since you seem to need it," he said, after what felt like the longest moment of her life.

Lynn nodded, her throat dry.

With that, Ryder Matthews turned and walked out of her office, but Lynn had the feeling he was coming back. She frowned and absently reached for her yogurt.

"Michelle," Lynn called, standing in front of the stove. "Call Jason home for dinner, would you?"

"Where is he?"

"Brad's...I think." She turned off the burner and opened the cupboard to take down the dinner plates. As a peace offering to her disgruntled son, Lynn was fixing his favorite meal. Tacos, with homemade banana cream pie for dessert.

Michelle finished making the phone call. "Brad's mom says he isn't there."

Lynn paused, distinctly remembering Jason telling her he was going to play at Brad's house. "Try the Sawyers' place then." Jason was sure to be there.

Michelle reached for the phone and hung up a minute later. "He's not there, either."

"He isn't in the yard, is he?"

"No," Michelle was quick to confirm. "I already checked there. Personally I think he needs to be taught a darn good lesson. I think we should just sit down and eat without him. He knew you were cooking dinner, and if he chooses to disappear, then let him go without."

"I planned tacos tonight just for him."

"All the better."

"Michelle, we're talking about an eight-year-old boy here."

"A *spoiled* eight-year-old boy."

Both Michelle and Jason were always so eager to see the other disciplined. Lynn prayed this was a stage her children were going through, because she found it downright irritating.

"Dinner's an effort to smooth his ruffled feathers for putting him in the day-care center. I don't want to use it against him."

"I'll see if he's at the Simons's," Michelle offered on the tail end of a frustrated sigh.

From the way her daughter walked toward the phone, Lynn could tell that Michelle heartily disapproved of her parenting techniques.

"While you're calling I'll check upstairs and see if he's there," she offered. It would be just like Jason to lie down and fall asleep while everyone was frantically searching for him.

The first thing Lynn noticed was that his bed was made and his room picked up. That in itself was a shock since she'd often claimed his room was a death trap and only Rambo himself would be brave enough to venture inside.

The note propped against his pillow caught her eye and she walked over to it. The few words seemed to leap off the paper and cut off her oxygen supply. Lynn read them nonstop twice. Her knees went so weak she had to reach out and grip the headboard to keep from falling.

"Jason isn't at the Simons's, either," she told Michelle as calmly as possible, once she returned to the kitchen.

"I know," Michelle said, impatiently. "I just got off the phone with Scott's mother. If you aren't going to take dinner away from him, I sincerely hope you punish him for this. I'm hungry, you know."

Lynn pulled out a chair and sat down. Her mind was whirling and she felt sick to her stomach.

"Where could that little brat be?"

"I...don't know," Lynn said, and her voice came out sounding like a rusty door hinge.

Michelle swung around, her eyes curious. With a trembling hand, Lynn handed her Jason's note.

"He's run away?" Michelle cried and her voice cracked. "My baby brother has run away?"

Five

The first thing Lynn did was phone the police station. Certainly they could tell her what to do in instances such as this. Although Lieutenant Anderson, the officer who answered her frantic call, was reassuring, he told her that until Jason had been missing twenty-four hours, there wasn't anything the authorities could do.

"Did he actually claim he was running away?" The lieutenant asked sympathetically.

Lynn's fingers tightened around Jason's carefully lettered note. "Not exactly...he said that I wouldn't need to worry about him anymore and that he could take care of himself."

Lieutenant Anderson's hesitation told Lynn everything she wanted to know. "I'm sorry, Mrs. Danfort, but there isn't anything more I can do."

"But he's only eight years old." Her voice wobbled as she struggled to hold back the fear. Lynn's imagination was tormenting her every minute that Jason was missing. Surely the men who had worked with Gary would be willing to do something to help her. Anything.

"I'm sure your son will be back before nightfall," the officer offered.

Lynn wasn't nearly as convinced. "But anything could happen to Jason in twenty-four hours' time. He's upset and angry... he could get into a car with a stranger... isn't there someone you could phone?''

Again the man hesitated. "I'll give the officers on patrol a description and ask them to keep an eye out for him."

Lynn sighed, grateful for that much. She wasn't sure Lieutenant Anderson would have been willing to do even that if he hadn't known Gary. "Thank you. I want you to know how much I appreciate this."

"No problem, Mrs. Danfort, but when you find Jason, call me."

"Yes," Lynn promised. "Right away." Her fingers felt like blocks of ice when she replaced the receiver. The chill extended down her arm and stopped at her heart. Lieutenant Anderson sounded so confident, as though eight-year-old boys ran away from home every day of the week. His attitude gave her the impression that as soon as Jason got hungry he would have a change of heart and head home. Maybe so, but it was a dark, cruel world out there and the thought of her son facing it alone frightened Lynn beyond anything else.

"Well?" Michelle asked, studying her mother once she'd finished talking to the police. "Are they forming a search party?"

Lynn shook her head. "Not yet."

"You mean they aren't going to bring in bloodhounds?"

"No."

"Oh, I guess they're right. Searchlights and helicopters will work much better since it's getting so close to nighttime."

"There aren't going to be any searchlights, or any helicopters."

"Good grief," the preteen shouted, obviously growing more agitated by the minute. "Exactly *what* are the authorities planning to do to find my baby brother?"

Damn little, but Lynn couldn't tell her daughter that. "The lieutenant promised to give Jason's description to the officers who are patrolling our area."

"That's it? That's the extent of their plans!" Michelle wore a shocked look.

Worry was clawing away at Lynn's insides.

"Mom," Michelle cried, "what are you going to do?"

Lynn wasn't sure. "I . . . I don't know." The lump in her throat felt as large as a Texas grapefruit as she desperately tried to force her mind into some type of positive action.

"Shouldn't we call someone?" Michelle suggested, tears brightening her eyes. "I could kill him, I could just kill Jason for this."

"It's the Peter Pan Day-care Center," Lynn said in a strangled voice that was barely above a whisper. He'd hated the idea from the very first, but she'd been forced to enroll him in a center that wasn't geared to a boy his age. There hadn't been anyplace else with openings.

Michelle's gaze was incredulous. "He wouldn't go there!"

Lynn stared at her daughter, wondering at Michelle's farfetched reasoning. The day-care center would be the last place Jason would think to hide. "Of course he wouldn't . . . don't be silly." Lynn's sense of panic was growing stronger each minute. "What about his friends?"

"I've already called everyone in the neighborhood," Michelle reasoned, rubbing her palms together and pacing the kitchen like a caged beast.

"What about Danny Thompson?" Lynn whispered, remembering a boy from school whom Jason had been thick friends with several weeks before school had been dismissed earlier in the month.

Michelle gnawed on her lower lip. "Nope, the Thompsons are on vacation, remember?"

Lynn vaguely did. "Michelle, think," she pleaded. "Where would he go?"

The girl shook her head, then shrugged her shoulders. "I swear to you, Mom, if you don't spank him for this, I will."

"Let's worry about punishing him once we find him." Although the need to shake some sense into her son *did* carry a strong appeal, Lynn kept her thoughts to herself.

"Uncle Ryder," Michelle shouted as though she'd just invented pizza. "I bet you anything, Jason contacted Ryder. Don't you remember...every other word out of his mouth for the past week has been Ryder this and Ryder that. He's been talking about him every day since the picnic."

"But Jason doesn't have any way of contacting Ryder," Lynn countered. "He doesn't know his phone number."

"Who says?"

Now that she thought about it, maybe Ryder *had* given Jason his phone number, but Lynn was sure Jason would have mentioned it earlier if Ryder had. He would have repeated every conversation at length, Lynn was convinced of that. No, Jason didn't have any way of getting in touch with Ryder—at least that she knew about.

"Mom, call Uncle Ryder," Michelle pleaded.

"But—"

"Mom, please, he could be our only hope!"

* * *

Ryder picked up the TV controller and absently flipped stations. Television really didn't interest him. Neither did dinner. His meeting with Lynn at noon hadn't gone well and he blamed himself. Lynn wasn't the same woman he remembered—for that matter, he wasn't the same man. She'd changed, matured, grown. In the past three years, she'd learned to deal effectively with the blows life had dealt her. She was competent and confident and stronger than he would ever have believed. That had pleased and surprised him. He'd been foolish to picture himself as a knight in shining armor, rushing to Seattle to rescue her from an unknown fate. Lynn didn't need anyone hurrying to her aid. She was doing just fine all on her own.

Another problem that Ryder had only now fully understood was that Lynn had always looked upon him as an endearing older brother. He knew she considered the thought of the two of them romantically involved as absurd. The idea of them kissing was downright incestuous. He supposed that was a natural response, after all, since they'd never viewed each other beyond good friends while Gary was alive.

Gary.

The role his former partner had played in his and Lynn's relationship presented an additional insight. Ryder had failed to realize that Gary had been the cohesive person in their friendship. Ryder had been Gary's partner and friend and Lynn had just been Gary's wife—at first. They'd eventually become fast friends as well, but Ryder was beginning to understand that, without Gary, that friendship had changed for Lynn. His three-year absence hadn't helped, either.

Ryder slouched back against the sofa and rubbed his hand across his face. He was expecting too much, too soon. All he had to do was give Lynn more time, and make himself available to her and the kids. He would invent excuses to drop by, win Lynn over little by little, until she was as comfortable with him as she had been in the old days. When the time was right to hold and kiss her, Ryder mused, he would be damned if Lynn treated him like a brother.

An idea started to form...a damn good one. A smile bounced from his eyes to his mouth, curving up the corners of his lips. Without realizing what he was doing, he stood and moved into the kitchen, unexpectedly ravenous. His hand was on the refrigerator when the telephone rang.

"Ryder," Lynn said, trying to control the anxiety in her voice. "I'm sorry to bother you..."

"Lynn, what is it?"

The alarm in Ryder's voice told her that no amount of fabricated poise was going to disguise the terror that had gripped her soul. She closed her eyes and slumped against the kitchen wall in an effort to compose herself before she started explaining Jason's note.

"Here," Michelle said, ripping the telephone out of her mother's hand. "Let me do the talking."

Lynn wasn't given an opportunity to protest.

"Uncle Ryder, this is Michelle," the youngster stated in a crisp, clear voice. "If you care anything at all about your godson then I suggest you get over here right away. Jason is missing and God only knows what's happened to him. He could be dead. Mother's in a panic, and frankly I'm upset myself." With that she replaced the receiver with a resounding force.

"Michelle," Lynn groaned. "That was a terrible thing to do to Ryder. He won't know what to think."

"What is there to think?" she demanded with irrefutable logic. "Jason's missing, we're worrying ourselves sick. Uncle Ryder is possibly the only man alive we know who can tell us what we should be doing to find that little monster."

"It still wasn't fair to frighten him like that," Lynn argued, reaching for the phone. She punched out his number and let it ring ten times before she hung up.

"He isn't going to take time to answer the stupid phone," Michelle stated the obvious. "Honestly, Mom, Ryder really cares about Jason and me."

That bit of dialogue threw Lynn for a spiraling loop. "How do you know that? Good heavens, you haven't seen him in years. I'm surprised you even remember him."

"Sure I do. Ryder always sends us nice Christmas gifts and he makes sure we hear from him on our birthdays."

"He's your godfather."

"I know. But I remember him from before..." She paused and a soft smile produced a dimple in both cheeks. "He used to sit me in his lap and tell me that I was going to grow up to be a princess someday. And if I was lucky, and he used to tell me that he was certain that I was very lucky, then I was going to be as pretty as my mommy."

"He told you that?"

Michelle nodded. "He used to make me laugh by telling me silly jokes, too." She hesitated and grinned. "I remember once that he told me that you can lead a horse to water but you can't teach him to do a handstand. I love Ryder. I'm glad he's back. It's almost like . . ." She paused and dropped her gaze, her expression sobering.

"Like what, honey?"

"Like the way things were before Dad died."

Michelle's words had a peculiar effect upon Lynn. She flinched as if stepping back to avoid an unexpected blow. Everything had been different since Gary's death. It was as if part of her had been waiting to wake up and discover the last three years had all been a nightmare. And yet so many positive things had happened in her life. She'd discovered herself, accepted her weaknesses, conquered numerous fears. On the negative side of Gary's death, she'd come to view the years she was married as idealistic, and that was a mistake. Her marriage hadn't been a stroll through Camelot, and it was wrong to compare every man she dated to Gary. Over the time he'd been gone, she'd found it increasingly difficult to imagine another man fitting into her and the children's lives. She wasn't a carefree teenager any longer. The ability to flirt and play cute were long gone. But if she was different, and she was, then so were men. Lynn hadn't been kidding when she told Toni Morris that the dating world was a jungle.

"I think I hear Ryder now," Michelle announced and raced out of the kitchen toward the front door. "Don't worry, if anyone can find Jason, he can."

Michelle was gone even before Lynn could stop her. The fact was, Lynn had trouble slowing down her own pace. She reached the door just in time to watch Michelle hurl herself into Ryder's arms and burst into flamboyant tears.

Ryder looked shocked by the preteen's emotional outburst. His gaze flew across the yard to Lynn who was standing on the front porch. One of her hands was braced against the wide support beam and the other hung limply at her side. In another time and place she would have wanted him to hold and reassure her too...but not now. She had to be strong, had to believe Jason would be found no worse for wear and everything was going to be all right. God wouldn't be so cruel that he would take both her husband and her son from her.

Ryder gently patted Michelle's back, and the tender way in which he spoke to the girl brought involuntary tears into Lynn's eyes. She looked away rather than let him know she was so close to weeping herself.

With one arm wrapped around Michelle's waist, Ryder led her to the top of the porch where Lynn was waiting.

"I can't seem to make much sense out of Michelle's story," he told Lynn. "Perhaps you'd better tell me what's going on with Jason."

Lynn opened her mouth to do exactly that, but when she started to speak, her voice cracked. Tears burned for release, tears she could barely control.

"He...I'm afraid Jason's decided to run away," she said and handed him her son's farewell note.

Six

Ryder took the creased note Lynn handed him and read the few short lines. "What did he take with him?"

Lynn's eyes rounded at the unexpected question. "I...I didn't think to check."

"Uncle Ryder, the police aren't doing anything to find Jason," Michelle informed him between loud sniffles. "No bloodhounds. No helicopter. No searchlights. Nothing."

"He'll need to be missing twenty-four hours before they get involved."

"I talked to Lou Anderson," Lynn explained, leading Ryder into the house and up the stairs to Jason's bedroom. "He's a lieutenant now and he was kind enough to give a description of Jason to the patrol officers, but I don't know if that'll do much good."

"It's something." Ryder paused just inside the bedroom door, surveying the room. "Did he pack any clothes?"

Systematically Lynn opened and closed her son's drawers, one after the other, until she'd finished with the chest. She couldn't see that he'd taken anything with him.

"I can tell you right now, he didn't bother with clean underwear," Michelle said with smug look. "If he brought anything it'd be those silly army things he treasures so much. He lives in those disgusting things. Mom practically has to wrestle him to the ground to get him to take 'em off so she can wash them.''

Ryder looked to Lynn, who nodded.

''Just a minute,'' Michelle cried, ''I just thought of something.'' Following that announcement, she raced down the stairs.

''Are you all right?'' Ryder asked Lynn in the same tender voice he'd used earlier with Michelle. She didn't know how to deal with this gentle, caring concern. Part of her wanted to lean on him and let him absorb some of this dreadful fear that attacked her common sense like fiery darts. Lou Anderson was probably right: Jason would be home as soon as he got hungry. But then there was the off chance that her son had stumbled into real trouble.

''I don't know what I feel,'' she answered and lifted her hand to brush aside a stray lock of hair. To add to her dismay, she noted that her fingers were trembling. ''I blame myself for this, Ryder. This is the first summer I haven't been home with the kids and it's been a disaster from the start. I don't know how other single parents manage home and a job. There've been so many problems.''

Ryder motioned for Lynn to sit on the edge of Jason's mattress and when she did, he sat beside her.

''I didn't have any choice,'' Lynn continued, staring straight ahead at the wall and the life-size poster of her son's idol, Sylvester Stallone. ''I had to enroll Jason in the Peter Pan Day-care Center. I couldn't leave Michelle and Jason by themselves.''

''I take it Jason isn't overly fond of Peter Pan's?''

''He hates it.'' She pinched her lips together as she remembered the martyred look he'd given her when she'd gone to pick him up that afternoon. It was enough to melt the hardest heart. "He . . . he would hardly talk to me on the way home. He claimed they made him eat tapioca pudding with a bunch of four-year-olds . . . his pride was shattered."

Ryder placed his arm over Lynn's shoulder and caressed the length of her upper arm in slow, even strokes that gently soothed her. The weight of his body, so close to her own, felt incredibly strong and confident. Without realizing what she was doing, she relaxed and had to fight the urge to rest her head against his shoulder.

"I've tried so hard to be a good mother, Ryder. I knew he was going to hate it there. I was trying to make it up to him by cooking his favorite dinner. He loves tacos and banana cream pie . . . I should have known that wouldn't be enough to appease him."

"You *are* a good mother, Lynn, don't be so hard on yourself."

"It's not only Jason running away," she admitted with a wobbly sigh. "The way he idolizes Rambo concerns me. That boy loves to wage wars—half the time he's living in a dream world in which he's the hero. Toni Morris told me it's a stage all little boys go through, but I can't help worrying. I can't help thinking—"

A breathless Michelle hurled herself into the room, interrupting Lynn. "I should have known," she announced dramatically. "The Oreos and a bunch of other goodies are missing, including a brand-new box of Cap'n Crunch cereal."

"He wouldn't think to take a sweater, but food didn't escape his notice," Lynn pointed out to Ryder.

"That thief took off with my fruit nuggets," an outraged Michelle continued.

"Your what?" Ryder's brow puckered with the question, obviously not understanding the significance.

"Fruit nuggets," Michelle repeated and slapped her hands against her sides in outrage. "Mother kindly explain!"

"It's a dried, gooey form of cherries, grapes, strawberries and other fruit that look like gumdrops."

"Ah."

"They were mine. Mom bought them for me and Jason knew it. That boy isn't any better than a . . . a . . ." Apparently Michelle couldn't think of anything low enough to compare him to. With her hands braced against her hips, the girl looked as outraged as if Jason had walked away with the national treasury stuffed into his pockets. A public hanging would be too good for him.

Ryder stood. "I think I've gleaned enough to know where he might be."

Apparently Ryder knew something Lynn didn't.

"Where?" Michelle demanded, noticeably eager to get her hands on her brother and her fruit nuggets while there was still time.

"I imagine he's taken along his backpack and his sleeping bag as well."

Michelle tossed open the closet door and peered inside. "Yup, both are missing."

Lynn leaped up and looked for herself. Sure enough, both were conspicuously absent.

"We've already phoned everyone in the entire neighborhood," Michelle advised Ryder. "I can guarantee you he isn't with any friends who live around here."

"I didn't think he would be."

"You'll call?" Lynn leaned against the closet door, her eyes wide and appealing.

"Every half hour, in case that boy's got the sense he was born with and decides to come home on his own. Otherwise I'll keep looking until he's found." His low voice was filled with an unwavering determination.

That lent Lynn some badly needed confidence. For the first time since finding Jason's note, Lynn felt a glimmer of reassurance.

"Ryder." The sound of his name vibrated in the air. He stopped abruptly and turned to her. Lynn held out her hand and grasped his fingers, squeezing them as hard as she could. "Thank you," she said in a strangled whisper. "I ... didn't know what to do or who to call."

He brushed his fingertips across her cheek in the briefest of touches. It was the touch of a man who would walk through hell to bring Jason back home. A shiver of awareness skidded down Lynn's spine and she managed a weak smile.

"Ryder will find him," Michelle murmured after he'd left. "I know he will."

"I do, too," Lynn answered.

The wooded area behind the local park was the logical place for Ryder to begin his search. From his experience earlier with his godson, Ryder remembered how much the boy loved exploring. He probably had a fort all prepared for this little exercise, and had thought most matters through before leaving home.

He quickly located several well-traveled paths that led deep into the thicket.

Within a matter of minutes, Ryder stumbled upon a fallen tree with a Star Wars sleeping bag securely tucked beneath a shelter that had been carefully dug out. A canteen rested beside that. Ryder checked the contents and when he discovered granulated cereal, he knew he'd found his prey.

All he had to do now was wait.

That didn't take long. About five minutes later, Jason came traipsing through the woods with a confidence his military hero would have envied. He stopped abruptly when he saw Ryder, his young face tightening.

"If you're here to take me home, I'm not going."

"Okay," Ryder agreed with an aloof shrug.

"You mean you aren't going to make me go back?"

Ryder shook his head. "Not unless that's what you want, and it's obvious to me that you don't." He straightened, stuck the tips of his fingers into his jeans pockets, and glanced around the campsite Jason had so carefully built. "Nice place you've got here."

Jason's eager grin revealed his pride. "Thanks. I'd offer you something to eat, but I don't know how long my food supply is going to last."

Once more Ryder shrugged and made a show of patting his stomach. "Don't worry about it, I'm saving my appetite for tacos and banana cream pie."

Jason's gaze shot up so fast it was a wonder he didn't dislocate his neck. "Tacos? Banana cream pie?"

"Smelled delicious, too."

Looking disconcerted, Jason swallowed and Ryder could have sworn the boy's mouth had started to water. In a gallant effort to disguise his distress, Jason walked over to the tree trunk and hopped onto the smooth bark. "I didn't want to have to run away like this, but Mom forced my hand."

"Peter Pan did it, right?"

"How'd you know?"

"Your mom told me about it."

"I suppose she sent you here."

"In a manner of speaking," Ryder answered smoothly. "She was pretty worried."

"I told her not to in my note," Jason fired back defensively. "Gee whiz, you'd think I couldn't take care of myself or something. That's the whole problem, Ryder, Mom treats me like I'm a little kid."

Ryder cast his eyes to the ground in order to hide his smile before Jason saw it. To his way of thinking an eight-year-old was a kid!

"I was planning to move back home as soon as school started, and the way I figure it, that's only six weeks. I've got to if I'm going to play with the Rockets."

"The Rockets?"

"My soccer team—we took first place last year. I made more goals than anyone, but Mom says it's a team sport and I can't take all the credit even though I worked the hardest and scored the most."

Feigning a pose of nonchalance, Ryder leaned against the fallen oak and crossed his arms and legs. "So Peter Pan's is the pits?"

"You wouldn't believe how bad it is. Half the time I was afraid some old lady was going to check me to see if I'd wet my pants."

"That bad?"

"Worse. It's unfair because Michelle gets to go over to her friend's house, but Mom sticks me in some kiddy factory." Jason drew a fruit nugget out of his pocket and popped it into his mouth, aggressively chewing it. "Mom's real nice and for a sister there are times when Michelle isn't half bad. The problem, the way I see it,

is that I'm surrounded by women who can't understand a man like me."

"I've had the same trouble myself," Ryder con-
fided.

His godson looked impressed. "I thought as much.
You were wearing a tortured look the day I saw you at
the lake."

"A tortured look?"

"Yeah, that's what I heard Mom say on the phone
once. She was talking to Mrs. Morris about a man she'd
gone out to dinner with and she said that and something else about him roaming the moors with Heath-
cliff...whatever that means."

Despite his effort not to, Ryder chuckled.

"Later, I asked Mom what she meant and she said
that he frowned a lot. You were frowning, too."

Ryder supposed that he *had* been scowling that day.
There'd been a good deal on his mind, not the least of
which was finding a way to approach Lynn after three
long years. He couldn't stroll up to a woman after that
length of time and casually announce he was in love
with her.

"I wanted to go to day camp with Brad—he's my best
buddy—they do neat stuff like horseback riding and
field trips, but Mom checked it out and they're already
full up." He reached for another fruit nugget, paused
and stared at it in the palm of his hand. "I don't suppose the banana cream pie was homemade?"

"It looked to me like it was."

Jason licked his lips. "I wonder if there were any
leftovers?"

"Oh, I'm sure there are. No one felt much like eating. Your mother was too upset and Michelle was crying."

"Michelle cried because of *me*?" Jason looked astounded. "But I took her fruit nuggets. Oh, I get it," he said, nodding vigorously. "She didn't know it yet."

"She noticed that first thing; there was something about the Oreos and some Cap'n Crunch cereal missing, too, now that I think about it."

"I have to eat, you know. I left Michelle the shredded wheat."

Ryder examined the end of his fingernails, pausing to clean beneath a couple before adding, "Don't worry, Michelle understands."

"Then why was she crying?"

"I don't completely understand it myself. She was sobbing so hard it was difficult to understand her, but from what I could gather, she was afraid something terrible could happen to you."

Jason lowered his gaze and rubbed his hands over the thigh of his army pants. "A drunk shouted at me, but I ran away from him...he didn't follow me, though, I made sure of that."

"I see."

Jason hesitated. "He might have seen which way I headed, though."

"That's a possibility," Ryder agreed.

Jason looked distinctly uncomfortable. "So you're sure Mom's all right."

"No, I can't say that she is. Your mother's a strong woman and it takes a lot to upset her, but you've managed to do that, son."

The boy's gaze plunged. "I suppose I should go home then...just so Mom won't worry."

"That sounds like a good idea to me. But before you do, I think we should have a talk—man to man."

* * *

Every minute that Ryder was gone felt like a lifetime to Lynn. She couldn't sit still, couldn't stay in one room, but paced between several. Not knowing what more she could do, she phoned everyone in the neighborhood and asked them to keep an eye out for Jason, although Michelle had already talked to all of Jason's friends. When she'd finished with that, she wandered back into her son's bedroom, but became so depressed and worried that she soon left.

Lynn was in the laundry room cleaning a cupboard when she heard Michelle's muffled cry. "Mom, Mom."

Dropping the rag, and rushing into the kitchen, Lynn discovered her daughter pointing to the inside of the junk drawer, tears raining down her face.

"What is it?"

"Jason left me a note," she sobbed. "He told me he was sorry for taking my fruit nuggets, but he needed them to live. He saved me all the grape ones . . . they're my favorite."

Lynn felt like bursting into tears herself.

"Ryder's going to find him."

Michelle had repeated those same words no less than fifteen times in the past hour. He hadn't phoned, which caused Lynn to be all the more nervous.

"I know." But the longer Ryder was gone, the less confident Lynn grew. Within an hour, she'd been reduced to cleaning cupboards.

Both Lynn and Michelle heard the car door slam from the driveway. Like a homing pigeon, Michelle flew to the living room window and pushed aside the drape.

"It's Jason and Ryder."

Lynn felt the weight of a hundred years lift from her shoulders. "Thank God," she whispered.

Seven

Jason walked into the house, his chin tucked so low against his shoulder that Lynn could see the crown of his head.

"Hello, Jason," she said, clenching her hands tightly together in front of her.

"Hi, Mom. Hi, Michelle."

Jason's voice was so low, Lynn had to strain to hear him speak.

Michelle sniffled loudly in a blatant effort to let her brother know how greatly he'd wronged her. She crossed her arms in an act of defiance, then whirled around, unwilling to face him or forgive him.

Ryder's hand rested on Jason's shoulder. "He was camping in the woods behind the park."

"The woods...behind the park," Lynn repeated, hardly able to believe what she was hearing. Even now the nightmares continued to ricochet off the edges of her mind. All the tragic could-have-beens pounded against her temple with agonizing force. If something had happened to Jason while he was hiding there, it could have been weeks before he was found.

"I believe Jason has something he'd like to say to you," Ryder continued.

The boy cleared his throat. "I'm real sorry for the worry I caused you, Mom."

Michelle whimpered softly.

"You, too, Michelle."

Somewhat appeased, the girl slowly turned to face her brother, amenable now to entertain thoughts of mercy.

"I promise I won't run away or hide or do anything like this ever again, and if I do, you can burn my army clothes and tear up my poster of Rambo." Having made such a gallant offer seemed to have drained Jason's energy bank. He paused, looked up at Ryder, who patted the boy's shoulder reassuringly and then continued. "I don't like that Peter Pan Day-care place, but I'm willing to stick it out until I go back to school. Next year we'll know to sign me up for day camp with Brad at the beginning of the summer so I can be with my best friend."

The knot in Lynn's throat felt as if it would choke her. The emotion that had blistered her soul demanded release. Heavy tears filled her eyes as she nodded, blurring her vision. Moisture ran down the side of her face and she held out her arms to her son.

Jason ran into them, his small body hurled against hers with enough force to knock her a step backward. He buried his face in her stomach and held on to her with such might that breathing was nearly impossible.

Michelle waited until Jason had finished hugging Lynn before she wrapped her arms around him in a rare display of affection. "You deserve the spanking of your life for this," she declared in high-pitched righteousness, "but I'm so glad you're back, I'm willing to let bygones be bygones . . . this once."

Jason tossed her a grateful glance. "Here," he said, digging his hands into his pockets. "I still got some of your fruit nuggets left."

Michelle looked down at the gooey, melting fruit pieces in his palm that had bits of grass and dirt stuck to them, wrinkled her nose and shook her head. "You can go ahead and eat them."

Jason was noticeably surprised. "Gee, thanks." He stuffed the entire handful into his mouth and chewed until a multicolored line of juice crept out of the corner of his lip. He abruptly wiped it aside with the sleeve of his shirt.

Michelle cringed. "You are so disgusting."

"What'd I do?" He asked and smeared more of the sugary fruit juice across his cheek.

Rolling her eyes, Michelle pointed toward the kitchen. "Go wash your hands and face before you touch something."

The pair disappeared and Lynn was left standing alone with Ryder. "I don't know how I can ever thank you," she told him. "I was so close to falling to pieces. When I found Jason's note it was like acid had burned a hole straight through me. I...I can bear just about anything but losing either of my children." She wiped the moisture from her cheekbones and tried to smile, failing. "I don't know how you guessed where he was hiding, but I'll always be grateful."

"I was here for you this time," he whispered.

"Oh, Ryder, don't blame yourself for the past. Please."

"I'm not. I went away because I had to, but I'm here now and if you've got a problem, I want to be the first one you call."

Lynn wasn't sure she understood his reasoning. He'd walked away from her when she'd needed him most and calmly strolled back into her life three years later, looking to rescue her. For the most part, Lynn didn't need anyone to save her, she'd managed nicely on her own. She was proud of her accomplishments, and rightly so. In the time since Gary's death, she'd come a long way with little more than occasional parental advice. If Ryder thought he could leap into her life, wearing a red cape and blue tights, then he was several years too late. She was about to explain that to him as subtly and gently as possible, when Jason stuck his head around the kitchen door.

"Can I have a taco and some pie?"

Between her relief that her son was all right and calling Lieutenant Anderson to tell him he'd been found, Lynn had completely forgotten dinner. "Ah . . . sure." She tossed a glance at Ryder. "Have you eaten?"

He grinned and shook his head.

"Then please join us. It's the least we can do to thank you."

Ryder followed her into the kitchen and while Lynn brought out the grated cheese, cubed tomatoes and picante sauce, Ryder helped Michelle and Jason set the table.

The easy friendship between Ryder and the kids amazed Lynn. It was as if he'd never been away. They joked and laughed together so naturally that she found it only a little short of amazing. Lynn didn't know of any male, other than the children's grandfather, that the kids seemed more at ease with.

With Jason safely home, the terrible tension had evaporated and dinner proved to be a fun, enjoyable meal. Lynn was convinced the reason Jason loved tacos so much was that he could make a mess without getting corrected for eating like a pig. Bits of fried hamburger, cheese and lettuce circled the area where he was eating. Blithely unaware, Jason downed three huge tacos and took seconds of pie.

"I'm a growing boy, you know," he told Lynn when he delivered his clean plate to the kitchen counter.

The phone rang and Michelle leaped upon it as if answering it before the second ring was a matter of life or death. "It's Marcy," she announced, pressing the receiver to her shoulder. "Can I go over to her house? She got a new tape she wants me to hear."

Lynn twisted around to look at the wall clock. "All right, but be back by eight."

"Mom, that's only a half hour."

"It's eight or not at all."

"All right, all right."

Jason yawned, covering his mouth with his palm, and after clearing the table, plopped himself down in front of the television. The next time Lynn glanced in his direction, her son was sound asleep.

"How about some coffee?" she asked Ryder.

"That sounds good."

He quickly loaded the dinner dishes into the dishwasher while Lynn started the coffee.

Lynn carried two steaming mugs into the living room where Ryder was waiting. He was standing in front of the television where a framed photograph of Gary rested. He turned, looking almost guilty, when she entered the room. He walked over to her to take one mug from her hand.

Her gaze skimmed across the photo of her late husband and back to Ryder. From the disconcerted look he wore, she knew he didn't want to discuss Gary, and she decided not to press the issue.

Smiling, she motioned for him to sit. He sat in the recliner and she took a seat on the sofa, slipping off her sandals and curling her feet beneath her.

"Well, this has certainly been an eventful day," she said, heaving a giant sigh. Rarely had any day been fuller or more traumatic. She'd effectively dealt with all the problems at work and had come home and faced even bigger ones there.

Ryder took a sip of the hot coffee. "It's been a good day for me. I'd forgotten how much I love Seattle. It feels right to be back here."

"It's good to have you." Lynn didn't realize how much she meant that until the words had already slipped from her lips. Ryder had always been a special kind of friend. For years she and Gary and Ryder had been thicker than thieves. Ryder was the brother Gary never had, and they were the best of friends. So Lynn's relationship with Ryder had fallen neatly into place because of his close association with her husband.

"I'm glad to be back, too." The color of Ryder's eyes intensified as his gaze held hers.

He dragged his look away with a reluctance she could feel all the way from the other side of the room. The undercurrents between them were so powerful that Lynn feared if she waded into anything beyond polite conversation, she would be pulled under and drown.

"Seattle's changed, though," he commented in a voice that was slightly husky. "I hardly recognized the downtown area for all the new construction."

"I saw from your business card that your office is on University Street. How does it feel to be a white-collar worker?" Her gaze moved from Gary's photo to Ryder.

"I don't know if I'll ever get used to wearing a tie every day. I'm more comfortable in Levi's than in a suit, but I suppose that'll come in time."

Lynn smiled, and talked about the many changes happening in the Seattle area. She was pleased that some of the old camaraderie between her and Ryder had returned. When Gary and Ryder had been partners, the three of them had often sat and chatted over a pot of coffee or a pitcher of beer. They'd camped together, hiked together, taken trips to Reno together. They attended concerts, cheered on the Seattle Seahawks and taken skiing classes together. More often than not they'd been a threesome, but every now and again, Ryder would include his latest love interest. Gary and Lynn had delighted in baiting Ryder about how short his "interest span" was when it came to any one woman. He'd responded to their teasing with good-natured humor. He liked to joke, saying he was trying to find someone who was as good a sport as Lynn but was not having any luck.

The three of them were comfortable together—there wasn't any need for pretense. When Michelle was born, Ryder had been her first visitor, arriving at the hospital even before the birth. When Gary and Lynn had asked him to be their daughter's godfather, Ryder's eyes had shone with such pride. He was as excited as Gary, carrying pictures of his goddaughter in his wallet and showing them to anyone who would stand still long enough to look. The case was the same with Jason. Ryder had been a natural with the kids, as good as Gary and just as patient and loving. Both Michelle and Jason had grown up with Ryder as a large part of their lives.

Then Gary had died and Ryder had abruptly moved away. Not only had Lynn lost her husband, but in one fell swoop, her two best friends as well.

Ryder must have read the confusion and doubt in her face because he started to frown. The television drew his gaze and his scowl deepened. He hesitated and then blurted out. "I had to leave in order to keep my sanity."

"Ryder, please, I understand. You don't need to explain."

"No, I don't think you do. Let me explain it one last time and then that'll be the end of it. My staying, continuing to be a part of your and the kids' lives would have been a constant reminder of Gary. Every time you looked at me, the memories would have been there slapping you in the face. You needed time to deal with your grief and I had to separate myself from you to get a grip on my own. Perhaps if I hadn't been with him that night...if the circumstances had been different, then the possibility of my remaining in Seattle would have been stronger. But I *was* there and it changed both our lives."

It was possible that Ryder was right, but Lynn didn't know anymore. She didn't want to think about the past and Ryder obviously found it equally painful.

"I'd been considering going back to law school even before...Gary died," Ryder confessed. "I think I may have even mentioned it at one point. I'd dropped out of graduate school in order to enter the academy because I wanted to make a more direct contribution to society. The idea of working with people, helping them, upholding law and order strongly appealed to me. At the time I couldn't see myself stuck away in some law office."

"You think you wasted your time on the force?" That would have surprised Lynn since she'd always assumed Ryder had loved his job as much as Gary had.

He shook his head. "I don't regret it at all. I saw where my effectiveness in a courtroom could be enhanced with my knowledge of police work. My parents had set aside a trust fund for me in case I *did* decide I wanted to go back to school. That had long been an option for me."

"And now you've achieved your goal," Lynn said and sipped her coffee. "I'm proud of you . . . you were always one to go after something when you wanted it. Gary was the same way. I think that's one reason you two were always such close friends—you were actually quite a bit alike."

"You share some of those character traits yourself."

He held himself rigid, refusing to relax. Their conversation was making him all the more uncomfortable, Lynn noted, and she knew all her talk about Gary was the cause.

"Tell me about Slender, Too."

She smiled at the question, knowing it was a blatant attempt to change the subject. She let him. "I've had the salon for about ten months. Buying that franchise was the scariest thing I've ever done, and I've managed to make a living with it, but it hasn't been easy."

"The kids seem to have adjusted to you working outside the home."

Lynn supposed they had, but the going hadn't been easy. Perhaps if she'd worked outside the home earlier in their lives Michelle and Jason might have adapted better. But they were accustomed to having her there when they needed her. The day-care problems this summer were a good example of how their lives had changed since she'd bought the business.

"If you run into any more problems, I want you to call me," he said, and straightened. He uncrossed his long legs and leaned forward, resting his elbows on his thighs.

"Ryder, I appreciate the offer, but there are few things I can't handle anymore."

"But there are some?"

She hesitated. After what had happened with Jason that evening, she didn't have a whole lot to brag about. "A few things every now and then."

"So call me and I'll do what I can to help straighten those things out."

"Ryder, honestly, you're beginning to sound like you want to be my fairy godfather."

He chuckled, but the sound quickly faded. "The last thing I want is for you to see me as an indulgent uncle."

His face and voice were fervent. It was the same expression he'd given her when they'd met at the precinct picnic, and she found it as disconcerting now as she had then.

Lynn was standing before she had a reason to be. Her mind searched for a logical excuse for why she'd found it necessary to bolt to her feet. The undercurrents tugging at her grew stronger. "Would you like some more coffee?" she asked, then her gaze rested on his still full mug.

"No, thanks."

Refilling her own mug justified the question, although hers was no closer to being empty than Ryder's, but she needed an excuse in order to escape.

Moving into the kitchen, she stood in front of the coffeepot. Lynn heard Ryder walk over and stand behind her. The warmth and proximity of his body were a distraction she chose to ignore.

He rested his hands on her shoulders and stroked her arms in a reassuring motion. "The past few years have been hard on you, haven't they?"

Lynn's hands were shaking as she lifted the glass pot and refilled her mug. "I've managed." Dear God, she mused, could that rickety, wobbly voice really be hers? Ryder may have said something more, Lynn didn't know. It took everything within her not to be conscious of the strength of his broad chest, which was pressing against her back. Perspiration beaded her upper lip and although she would have liked to blame it on the heat, the day had actually been cloudy with the temperature in the low seventies.

"Lynn, turn around."

Reluctantly she did what he asked, all the while conscious of how close they were.

With a deliberate action, Ryder removed the mug from her fingers and set it aside. Lynn felt as if she were in a daze, hypnotized and immobile. Anytime else, with anyone else, she would have demanded to know the other person's intentions. But not with Ryder.

She knew what he wanted.

That knowledge would have troubled her except that she was honest enough to admit she wanted it, too.

He placed his hands on her shoulders once more, and his touch so confused her senses that voicing her thoughts became impossible. He slowly glided his fingers over her face, down her cheek to her neck. He reached for the French braid, which fell down the middle of her back, and pulled it free, easing his hands through it. His gentle stroke was that of a lover, appreciating a woman's beauty.

Lynn's breath jammed in her throat and her heart started beating like a rampaging herd of buffalo. She refused to look up at him, concentrating instead on the buttons of his shirt because it was safe to look there.

"Lynn."

The demand in his voice was unmistakable. She had to glance up, had to meet his eyes. When she did, she couldn't stop staring at him. They were so close she could see every line in his rugged features. His nostrils flared slightly and the action excited her more than his touch had. Sexual excitement and longing, which had been dormant for years, filled her. The feelings felt foreign and yet perfectly natural.

He lowered his lips to hers.

Slowly, moving as though directed by Ryder's thoughts, hypnotized by what she witnessed in his eyes, Lynn moved in his arms, going up on her tiptoes, raising one hand to clench his shoulder for support.

He brushed his mouth against hers, softly, tenderly, in a butterfly kiss that teased and tantalized her. Her lips trembled at the swell of pure sensation. A soft rasping breath escaped, but Lynn didn't know if it came from her or Ryder. Her eyes were closed, blocking out reality, excluding everything but this incredible whitecap of sensation that had lapped over her. She wanted to deny these sensations, but it was more than she was capable of doing in that moment—more than Ryder would allow.

Still trembling, Lynn repositioned her upper body, hoping to escape his arms. She soon realized her mistake as the softness of her breasts grazed the hard wall of his chest.

Ryder's breath caught as her hardened nipples nuzzled against him. While once she'd sought to move away, now her arms slid around his neck.

He kissed her then, the way a starving man samples his first bite of food. His tongue and lips alternately plundered and caressed, tasting, savoring, relishing her mouth until they were both breathless. Gasping, Lynn met his ravishing hunger with her own powerful need. She was shaking so hard that if he were to release her, she was convinced she would collapse onto the floor.

Passion built between them until Lynn felt as though her soul had been seared by the magnitude of their kissing and touching.

His mouth left hers to slide across her cheek to her ear. An involuntary moan escaped as he nibbled her lobe.

"How I've dreamed of holding you like this," he murmured, his voice husky and low. His breath felt warm and moist against her skin.

The front door slammed and the sound reverberated around the kitchen like a ricocheting bullet. Lynn broke away from Ryder so fast that she would have tumbled if he hadn't secured her shoulders. Once he was assured that she was stable, he released her, dropping his hands to his sides.

"I'm back," Michelle announced, racing into the kitchen with the fervor of a summer squall.

For some obscure reason, Lynn felt it essential to reach for her coffee. She took a sip and in the process nearly spilled the entire contents down her front.

Michelle stopped abruptly and looked from Ryder to her mother and then back to Ryder. "I'm not interrupting anything, am I?"

"No...of course not," Lynn said quickly. The words stumbled over her tongue like rocks crashing off the edge of a cliff and bouncing against the hillside on the long tumble downward.

"Your mother and I would like a few minutes alone," Ryder inserted, staring straight through Lynn.

"Oh, sure."

Michelle had turned and started to walk out of the room when Lynn cried. "No...don't go...it's not necessary." She knew she was contradicting Ryder, but now in the harsh light of reality, she felt ashamed by the way she'd succumbed to his kissing. She awkwardly struggled to rebraid her hair.

Michelle was noticeably confused. Her gaze jerked from her mother back to Ryder. "I wanted to show Marcy my *Teen* magazine. We were going to go up to my room. That's all right, isn't it? She's asking her mom now if she can come over here."

It took Lynn a full minute to decide. With Michelle gone, she would have to face Ryder alone and she didn't know if she could bear to look him in the eye. She'd behaved like a love-starved creature, giving in to him in ways that made her blush all the way to the marrow of her bones. She'd clung to him, kissed him with an abandon that made her feel weak at the memory.

"Mom?"

"Ah...sure, that's fine."

Michelle gave her an odd look. "Are you all right?"

"Of course," she answered in a falsely cheerful voice.

"You look all pale, like you did when you came downstairs with Jason's note." The girl's gaze narrowed. "He hasn't run away again, has he? That little brat...I knew I was being too generous to forgive him so easily."

"He fell asleep in front of the television," Ryder answered for her. "I don't think you'll have any more problems with him running off."

"It's a good thing you talked to him, Ryder. Someone had to. Mom tries, but she's much too easy on that boy. Mothers tend to be too softhearted."

The doorbell chimed and Michelle brightened. "That's Marcy now."

She ran to answer the door, and rather than face Ryder, Lynn walked away from him and into the family room where Jason lay curled up on the sofa, sound asleep.

"Jason," she whispered, nudging him gently. "Wake up, honey."

"He's dog tired," Ryder said when Jason grumbled and rolled over in an effort to ignore his mother's voice. "Let him sleep."

"I will once I get him upstairs," she said. Her heart began to pound against her ribs in slow, painful thuds. It took all the courage she could muster just to look in Ryder's direction.

"Here," Ryder said, stepping in front of her. With strength she could only envy, he lifted the sleeping boy into his arms and headed for the staircase.

Jason flung his arms out and lifted his head. He opened his eyes just enough to look up and assess what was happening.

"Your mother wants you upstairs," Ryder explained.

Jason nodded, then closed his eyes, content to let Ryder carry him. That in itself told Lynn how exhausted her son was. From what she'd learned over dinner, Jason had been planning his escape for several days. The boy probably hadn't had a decent sleep in two or three nights.

Lynn walked up the stairs behind the two; all the while her heart was hammering with trepidation. Once Jason was tucked into his bed, her excuses would have run out and she would be forced to face Ryder. It wasn't likely that she was going to be able to avoid him. She could try to lure Michelle and her friend into the kitchen, but Lynn wasn't likely to interest them in coming downstairs when there was a *Teen* magazine clenched in their hot little hands.

Ryder set Jason on the edge of his mattress and peeled off the boy's shirt.

"He should probably take a bath."

"Ah, Mom," Jason grumbled, and yawned loud enough to wake people in three states. "I promise I'll take one in the morning." He made a gallant effort to keep his head up, but it lobbed to the side as if it had suddenly become too heavy for him to support.

"A bath in the morning," Lynn muttered under her breath. "Those are famous last words if I ever heard them."

Ryder shared a grin with her and the simple action went a long way toward easing some of the tension that was crippling her.

Next Ryder took off Jason's tennis shoes. A pile of dirt fell to the floor as the first sneaker was removed from the boy's foot.

"If Michelle were here, she'd be screaming, 'oh, yuck.'" Lynn joked in an effort to ease more of the tension.

Soon Jason was in his pajamas. He didn't hesitate in the least before climbing between the sheets. He curled up in a tight ball, wrapping his arms around his pillow as though it were a long lost friend and they'd just recently been reunited.

"He won't wake up till morning," Ryder said, and gently smoothed the hair at the top of her son's head.

"Do you want any more coffee?" Lynn asked, on her way out of the bedroom.

"No."

She was so grateful she actually sighed with relief. Maybe he would decide to go home and give her the space she needed to think. Her thoughts were like murky waters and had clouded her reasoning ability. Kissing Ryder had been curious enough, but to become a wanton in his arms was something else entirely.

He waited until they were back in the kitchen before he spoke. "I don't want coffee or dessert. You know what I want." His voice was so low and seductive that just the sound of it caused tiny goose bumps to break out over her arms.

"Ryder..." She meant to protest, to say something—anything that would put an end to this madness. But Ryder didn't give her the opportunity. Before she could object, he turned her into his arms. Any opposition she'd felt earlier disappeared, like snow melting under an August sun, the minute he reached for her.

Ryder's arms closed convulsively around her waist.

"Please...don't."

"I've waited too long to go back now."

Lynn didn't understand any of what was happening, but when Ryder reached for her, she couldn't find it within herself to resist. His mouth swooped down on hers, his kiss possessive and hard, and yet incredibly soft. His tongue slid into her mouth and moved leisurely, stroking her own. Against every dictate of her will, Lynn lifted her arms to encircle his neck, and shamelessly gave herself over to his kiss.

Ryder groaned.

Lynn whimpered.

He kissed her again and again with a thoroughness that left her shivering, as if in a single minute he wanted to make up to her for all the years they'd been apart.

He gripped her hips, dragging her infinitely closer to him. She balked when she felt the evidence of his arousal. From somewhere deep inside she found the effort to resist.

"No," she cried. "Please...no more." She twisted her face away from him and buried it in his shoulder.

"Lynn..."

"I...think you should go home now."

"Not until we've talked."

"But we're not talking now and I don't know what's happening between us. I need time to think. Please...just go. We'll talk, I promise, but later." Lynn had never felt more unsettled about anything in her life.

He hesitated. He gently stroked her hair as though he had to keep touching her. "It's too soon, isn't it?"

"Yes," she cried. She didn't know if that were true, but was willing to leap upon any excuse.

Slowly, as though it was causing him pain to do so, Ryder dropped his arms and stepped away from her.

A chill descended upon her as he moved away and she lifted her arms, cradling them around her waist.

"I'll be back, you know," he whispered. "And next time, I won't be willing to listen to any excuses."

Eight

"This is a rare treat," Toni Morris said when Lynn slid into the booth across from her in the seafood restaurant close to Lynn's salon. "It's been months since we last had lunch together."

Lynn's smile was noticeably absent as she picked up the menu and glanced over the day's luncheon specials. She decided quickly upon a Crab Louie and spent the next several minutes adjusting the linen napkin on her lap.

"Well," Toni said, propping her elbows atop the table and lacing her fingers, "are you going to come right out and tell me why you arranged this meeting or are you going to keep me in suspense for half the meal?"

Lynn should have known Toni would see through this luncheon invitation. "What makes you think there's something I want to talk about?"

Toni grinned, the simple action denting dimples in both cheeks. The thing Lynn found amazing about this former policewoman was her ability to be both tough and tender. She could look someone in the eye, cut them to the quick with her honesty and then heal them with a smile.

"You mean other than the fact you phoned me at ten-thirty last night suggesting we meet?"

Lynn's gaze darted past her friend. "It was a bit late, wasn't it?"

"Don't worry, you didn't get me out of bed."

The waitress came to take their order and Lynn was given a few minutes respite. She'd wanted to gradually introduce the subject of Ryder, but her friend wasn't going to allow that, which was probably best. Left to her own devices, Lynn was likely to avoid anything that had to do with the man until the last ten minutes of their lunch.

"Ryder came by last night," she said in as normal a tone as she could manage. "Actually I phoned him, desperate because Jason had run away and I thought he might have contacted Ryder."

"Jason did *what*?"

"You heard me right...he hates Peter Pan's so much that he decided to live in the woods behind the park until soccer practice started the first week of September and then come home."

Momentarily speechless, Toni shook her head and reached for a bread stick. "That child amazes even me."

"I called Ryder and he found Jason for me."

"How?"

"God only knows. I called him because...well because Jason mentioned Ryder's name every ten seconds after they met at the precinct picnic and I thought Ryder might know where Jason was hiding. Actually Michelle had insisted. By the time he arrived I was a candidate for the loony bin."

"I don't blame you. Good grief, Lynn, you should have let me know."

"There wasn't anything you could have done. I called the station and talked to Lou Anderson. You know him, don't you?"

"Yes, yes, go on—how did Ryder know where to find Jason?"

"It was a matter of simple deduction. Unfortunately I was in too much of a panic to think straight at the time. Ryder arrived, asked several pertinent questions and used simple logic. Once Ryder went looking for him, Jason was home within the hour."

"Thank God." Toni expelled a tight sigh. "That boy is something else."

"Tell me about it." Lynn lowered her gaze and nervously smoothed an already creaseless napkin. "Ryder stayed for dinner and later we talked and..." A lump of nervous anticipation blocked her throat. It was one thing to tell her friend that Ryder had kissed her and another to admit how strongly she'd reacted to it.

"And what? For heaven's sake, woman, spit it out."

Despite everything, Lynn laughed.

"You want me to help you out?" Toni joked. "Ryder came over, found Jason, stayed for dinner and the two of you talked. Okay, let's go from there. Knowing you both the way I do, I'd guess that Ryder kissed you and you went into a tizzy."

Lynn nearly swallowed her glass of ice tea whole because Toni was so close to the truth. "How'd you know?"

Toni waved a bread stick like a band leader wielding a baton. "Let's just say I'm not the only one able to deduce matters from the evidence presented me."

Shaken, Lynn stared at her friend, wondering how much more Toni had guessed. She looked amazingly pleased by what had happened, as though she'd orchestrated the entire event herself.

"But Ryder isn't the first man to kiss you in the past three years." Toni's curious smile deepened, causing the edges of her mouth to quiver slightly.

"No, he isn't," Lynn admitted, "but he's the first one who's made me feel again. He appears to want to make up to me for the years he was away, insisting I call him when I stumble into any roadblocks. He doesn't seem to understand that I've changed and when something bothersome crops up, I prefer to find my own solutions."

"He's changed, too, you know."

"But I fear his concern for me and the kids is motivated by guilt."

"The kiss, too?"

"I...I don't know," Lynn answered, wavering. "He came by the salon yesterday, wanting to take me to lunch. I turned him down."

"Why?"

"For the same reasons I didn't want to have dinner with him when he suggested it at the picnic."

"Which are?"

"Oh, Toni, stop. You know as well as I do that I just don't have time right now for a social life. Good heavens I probably shouldn't even be taking a whole hour for lunch today. This summer's been hectic at the salon, I can't seem to find good permanent help. The new girl phoned in and said she wouldn't be able to make her shift—she didn't even bother to give me an excuse. I think she'd rather be at the beach. I suspect the only reason she took the job in the first place was to tone up her muscles and get paid for it at the same time. It's been one problem after another for the past three weeks."

Toni's eyes grew serious. "Those are all excuses not to see Ryder and you know it."

"It isn't!"

"Ryder loves you . . ."

"We're friends—that's all. If he feels anything toward me it's rooted in his relationship with Gary. He helped me yesterday when Jason disappeared, like an older brother would help a younger sister."

"Is that the way he kissed you? Like a brother?"

Toni's words whooshed the argument out of Lynn like hot air from a balloon and with it went all pretense. "No, and that's what concerns me most."

"In other words, it felt good."

"*Too* good," she admitted in a tight whisper. "Much too good."

Their salads arrived and Lynn looked down at the lettuce covered with fresh crab meat and realized her appetite had vanished. She picked up her fork, but after a couple of moments, set it back down again. When she looked up, she noticed that Toni was watching her, her friend's eyes revealing her concern.

"It isn't the end of the world to like it when a man kisses you," Toni said with perfect logic. "If the truth be known, I've been worried about you lately. You've been so involved with Slender, Too, working far harder than you should have to, in addition to keeping up with the kids and the house. Something's going to have to give soon."

"Like my sanity?" Lynn tossed out the words jokingly, but actually she wasn't so far off base. It was the only rational way she could explain what had happened between her and Ryder. For the past year, she'd been dating occasionally, but no one had made her feel the way Ryder did. It had been months since a man had touched her. Months since she'd allowed her body to feel anything sexual. Just the memory of the way Ryder's hands had felt against her shoulders and back, the way he'd run his long, strong fingers through her hair, caused a rush of sensation shooting all the way down to her toes.

"Ryder cares about you and the kids," Toni said, still looking thoughtful and disturbed.

Lynn didn't want to hear that, not because she didn't believe it, but for the other reasons. "He thinks he can leap into my life after three years as if... as if nothing had ever happened."

"I don't think that's his intention."

"Well, I do!" Lynn flared. Toni chose to ignore her short temper, Lynn noted, and took a bite of her salad before answering. "Then what do you think?"

"I can only guess at what Ryder intends. If it bothers you so much, why don't you ask him?"

Toni's question hung between them.

"But one word of warning, my friend," she added softly, "be prepared for the answer."

"What do you mean by that?"

"Just that I know you both. Ryder didn't come back here by accident—he planned it."

"Of course he did. He was accepted into a law firm in Seattle. He's familiar with the courts here and police procedure. It only makes sense that he'd want to set up his practice in this area."

"Yes, it *does* make sense, but for other reasons, too."

"Right," Lynn answered defiantly. "He seems to think I need to be saved from myself and I find that both insulting and irritating. His whole attitude suggests I've bungled my family's lives for the past three years, and that everything's going to be better now that he's back. Well, I've got news for Ryder Matthews. *Big news.* I got along without him then and I can do it now.''

Toni didn't say anything for several tortuous moments. ''Don't you think you're confusing two separate issues?''

''No.'' Lynn answered without giving the question adequate thought. ''He was a friend—a good one, and he feels a certain amount of guilt over what happened. If Ryder came back for any specific reason, it was to purge himself from that.''

Toni arched her finely penciled brows. ''I see. Then you have all the answers.''

Not quite, but Lynn wasn't sure she was ready to admit as much. ''I think I do.''

''Then Ryder's task is going to be more difficult than he imagined.''

''What do you mean?''

Toni glanced at her watch and sighed. ''Listen, I'd like to stay and talk, but I promised to meet Joe. He wants to look at lawn mowers during his break.'' She offered Lynn a cocky smile and murmured, ''From the sounds of it, you've got everything figured out, anyway.''

''I...I don't know that I do.'' That was more difficult to admit than Lynn cared to think about. She knew Ryder, she knew herself, but they'd both changed.

''You'll figure everything out—just give yourself time.'' Toni set her napkin beside her plate and reached for the tab, studying it before retrieving her wallet. ''I will make one suggestion, though.''

''Sure.''

''The next time Ryder stops by, ask him why he moved back to Seattle. You might be surprised by the answer." Following that, she scooted out of the seat and was gone.

By the time Lynn returned to the salon, she was more confused than ever. She'd wanted to talk out her feelings to Toni, but something had gone awry. It took her a while to realize what. Secretly Lynn had wanted Toni to tell her that kissing Ryder was all wrong. She'd hoped her friend would explain that she and Ryder had marched neglectfully into an uncharted area in a relationship that was best left alone. Unfortunately, Toni hadn't. Instead her friend had thrown questions at her Lynn didn't want to answer.

Lynn was forced to acknowledge that whatever her relationship had been with Ryder before he moved to Boston, it had now been altered. That much had been obvious from the minute she saw him at the picnic. Only it had taken time for Lynn to recognize that. She and Ryder weren't going to slip back into those old familiar roles, although Lynn would have been content to do so.

With her not-so-subtle questions, Toni kept insisting Lynn own up to her own feelings, which at the moment were difficult to decipher. Okay, so Ryder's kiss had affected her. She would figure out why and that should be the end of it.

Sharon walked into the office almost as soon as Lynn arrived. "Carrie phoned after you left. She won't be able to come in today."

Lynn groaned inwardly. "Is she sick?"

"She claims she was up half the night with some flu bug."

Lynn slouched down into her chair and released a frustrated sigh. "Great."

"Do you want to toss a coin and see which one of us stays until eight?"

Lynn was touched by her assistant's generosity. "No, I'll do it."

"What about Michelle and Jason?"

Lynn shrugged, there wasn't anything else to do. "I'll pick them up at four. They'll just have to stay here with me until closing time."

Sharon chuckled. "Jason's going to love that. Can't you just see him down here with his toy machine gun, waving it at all these women in fancy tights?"

"I'll keep him busy drawing pictures in my office." That was optimistic thinking in action.

Sharon regarded her silently for a long moment. "You're sure? I can probably make arrangements with my sitter, if you want."

"No, I'll do it. Thanks anyway." It was her business and she was the one responsible. Besides, Sharon had stayed late one night this week already and Lynn couldn't ask that of her a second time.

"Okay, if you're sure." Sharon looked doubtful.

"I am. Were there any other calls?"

"Yeah, that guy with the sexy voice phoned ten minutes after you left. He asked that you return his call and gave me the number. It's on your desk."

So Ryder had contacted her at lunchtime—somehow Lynn had expected he would.

"Anything else happen?"

"Not much. There were two or three more calls; I left the messages on your desk."

"Thanks, Sharon."

"No problem, it's what you pay me for."

Lynn sorted through the pink slips that were on top of her desk. She found it interesting that Sharon would specifically mention Ryder's call, but none of the others—except Carrie's.

From dealing with Ryder in the past, Lynn knew if she didn't return his call, he would keep trying until she answered. It was best to deal with him when she was the most prepared. Besides, she already knew what he wanted—he'd told her so himself when he'd left her the night before. He wanted to talk. Well, she didn't and she planned on telling him as much.

With resolve straightening her backbone, Lynn punched out his telephone number and waited. A secretary answered, her husky voice cool and efficient, conjuring up pictures of someone young and attractive. A pang of jealousy speared its way through Lynn. She found the emotion completely ridiculous. Ryder could be working with Miss World for all she cared.

"Ryder Matthews."

"Ryder, it's Lynn. I got the message that you called."

"Yes. I checked out a couple of day camps and found one in your area with an opening. Ever hear of Camp Puyallup?"

Lynn was so astonished it took her a full moment to find her breath. "Of course I have. It's the camp Jason wanted to attend, but they were full . . . I checked it out myself. Jason's friend Brad goes there."

"There's an opening now if Jason's interested."

"But . . . we're on their waiting list, we were told it wasn't likely that he'd get in this summer. How did you manage it?"

Ryder hesitated as if he didn't want to admit something. "I phoned first thing this morning and was able to pull a few strings."

Lynn didn't know whether she should be furious or overjoyed. She knew how *Jason* would react, however, Her son would be in seventh heaven at the thought of escaping Peter Pan's. Lynn supposed she should be grateful Ryder had intervened on her behalf, but she didn't like him stepping into her life and "pulling strings." She could find her own solutions. All right, this day-care problem with Jason had been a thorn in her side and her son's as well.

"Jason will be pleased." It took an incredible amount of discipline to tell Ryder that much, although she tried to let him know in the cool way in which she spoke that she didn't appreciate what he'd done.

The ensuing silence was loud enough to create a sonic boom.

"I didn't mean to offend you." It was apparent from the clipped way in which he released his words that Ryder was upset. "I was only trying to help, Lynn."

"I know." She closed her eyes and let out a ragged sigh. It would be ridiculous to punish Jason because of her foolish pride. He was miserable at the center where he attended now and Camp Puyallup would be perfect for him.

"The camp director wanted to meet Jason tonight. Could you stop by with him for a few minutes after work?"

Lynn felt like weeping. "I can't...not tonight." As it was, her schedule was going to be exceptionally tight. She would barely have time to pick up Jason and Michelle and be back at the salon in time to lead Carrie's four-thirty aerobics class.

"You can't take Jason! Why not?"

"I've got to work late. In fact, I was going to bring the kids down here with me."

"For how long?"

"Until closing."

"Which is?"

"Eight." It sounded like an eternity to Lynn. She could just see herself leading a dance aerobics class and trying to keep Jason out of mischief all at the same time. Tonight was going to be "one of those nights."

"Then I'll take Jason down myself," Ryder offered. "In fact, I'll pick up both kids; we'll make a night of it. I'll treat them to dinner and a movie afterward."

"Ryder, no. That isn't necessary."

"You'd rather have both kids down there with you? They'll be bored stiff."

Lynn didn't have any argument. Ryder was right. Given the choice between going to dinner and a movie with Ryder and staying holed up in her office, Lynn knew who the kids would want to spend the evening with. And she couldn't blame them.

"Well?"

"I . . . suppose that would be all right. I'll call Peter Pan's and tell them you'll be by to pick up Jason. Michelle's spending the day with Marcy . . . you met her last night."

"What time will you be home?"

"As soon after eight as I can manage."

Another silence followed, and Lynn was convinced Ryder was debating on whether to say something about the long hours she was putting in. She was grateful when he didn't.

"I'll have the kids home about that time."

"It's good of you to do this, Ryder. I appreciate it."

She could feel his smile all the way through the telephone line. "That wasn't so hard, was it?" he asked in a light teasing voice that was mellow enough to melt her insides.

It was apparent that he hadn't a clue as to how difficult it had been.

* * *

Ryder set down the phone and grinned lazily. He leaned back in his swivel chair and cupped his hands behind his head, satisfied by this unexpected turn of events. He was going to see Lynn again far sooner than he'd anticipated and that pleased him immeasurably.

Lynn had amazed him on two accounts. The first and foremost had been the way in which she'd responded to his kiss the night before. The plain and simple truth was that for the past six months, Ryder had been living on the edge. His biggest fear was that Lynn was going to meet another man and fall in love before he could get back to Seattle. He hadn't been eating properly—nor had he been sleeping well. There were so many hurdles to leap when it came to loving Lynn that fear had crowded his heart and his mind.

But holding and kissing her had sent him sailing over the first series of obstacles without a problem. She couldn't have responded to him the way she did without feeling something—and it wasn't anything remotely related to a brotherly affection. She'd wanted him. Ryder could feel it in his bones.

He hadn't been able to sleep for long hours afterward. Every time he closed his eyes, he imagined tasting her sweet mouth, filling his palms with her perfect breasts and caressing her creamy thighs. If she'd wanted him to make love to her, and Ryder knew she did, it only touched the surface of the desire he'd experienced for her. By the time he arrived back at his apartment, his whole body had ached with the need she'd inflicted upon him.

Months ago, when Ryder had first realized he was in love with Lynn, his first fleeting reaction was that it was wrong to feel the way he did. The best thing was for him to stay out of her life and let her find happiness elsewhere. It didn't take him much time to realize he couldn't allow that to happen. Like it or not Lynn was a part of him, and releasing her to love another man would be like chopping off his own arm. He could have managed it, but he would have gone through the remainder of his life aching his loss. Last night had confirmed that he'd made the right decision to woo Lynn. She was going to love him and the knowledge was enough to make him want to stand on top of his desk and shout for joy.

The second way in which Lynn had surprised him was how promptly she'd returned his phone call. It was almost as if she'd been eager to talk to him. Unfortunately, Ryder knew otherwise. He'd heard it in the sound of her voice, the minute he'd picked up the phone. She'd wanted to deal with his call and be done with it. Under different circumstances, Ryder would have been prepared for a two- or three-day wait for her to contact him. He didn't have time to delay and would have phoned her again until he reached her, but she'd surprised him first. Ryder didn't doubt that Lynn had been frustrated and confused over their encounter in her kitchen the night before. Talking to him would be the last thing she wanted to do, but she'd taken the initiative and he was proud of her.

Over the years, Ryder had learned to cherish his independence, and he could well appreciate Lynn's needs in that area. But damn it all, she couldn't manage everything on her own. It was time she set aside her pride and accept his willingness to lend her a helping hand.

She needed him just as much as he needed her.

Nine

Silence yawned through the living room when Lynn let herself into the house. Exhausted, she looped her purse on the doorknob to the entryway closet and walked directly into the kitchen. Usually she led two aerobics classes in a single workday, but on this one, she'd been forced to do four twenty-minute dance sessions. Every muscle in her weary body was loudly voicing its objection to the strenuous activity.

Lynn groaned when she stepped into the kitchen, rotating her neck to ease the stiffness there. The place was a disaster. As an experiment, Lynn had given Michelle a key to the house so her daughter could come and go as she pleased.

That was a mistake. From the looks of it, Michelle had decided to bake something. Now that she thought about it, she vaguely remembered Michelle phoning to ask permission to mix dough for chocolate-chip cookies. The entire conversation remained blurry in her mind, but from what she recalled, the actual baking part would take place at Marcy's house.

A fine dusting of flour littered the countertops like frost on a winter's morning. The sugar bowl was open and chocolate chips were scattered from one end of the kitchen to the other.

Lynn popped a chocolate morsel into her mouth and let it melt on her tongue. It tasted incredibly good. She was beyond hungry—she'd barely touched her crab salad at lunch and it was hours past dinnertime.

It was after she'd finished wiping down the counters that Lynn found her daughter's note, promising to clean up the kitchen once she got home. Tiny print at the bottom of the page informed Lynn that her daughter had hidden her share of the cookies from Jason, they were somewhere safe in the house and Michelle would get one for her when she was home from the movie.

Opening the freezer door, Lynn found a TV dinner, and after reading the cooking directions, set it inside the microwave.

Seven minutes sounded like an eternity as she plopped herself down in the living room, removed her tennis shoes and stretched her feet on top of the ottoman. If she could only close her eyes for a moment and rest...for just a minute.

Indistinctly, as if it were coming from a great distance, she heard the timer on the microwave beep. She didn't have the energy to move.

"Mom."

Lynn bolted awake, her feet dropping to the floor with a thunderous thud.

"Mom, guess what?" Jason flew into the room at the speed of a charging elephant, carrying with him—of all things—a stuffed furry basketball. "Ryder took me over to Camp Puyallup and I met everyone and they said I could join their troop. Brad and me are going to be partners tomorrow. Isn't that the greatest thing since...since hand grenades?"

Lynn managed to smile through her brain fog. "That's...wonderful, Jason."

"It's more than great . . . it's hell good."

"Hell good?"

"That's what everyone says when something is stupendous," Michelle informed her mother.

"I see." Lynn rubbed a hand over her face to wipe the sleep out of her eyes, hoping the action would unclog her mind. When she looked up Ryder was standing there, staring down on her. He was impossibly handsome and when he grinned, deep grooves formed at the sides of his mouth. Lynn felt as if the sun had come out and bathed her in its warm light. His smile was designed to disarm her and, to her chagrin, he succeeded. She smiled back despite her best intentions to cool things between them. She hated to admit, even to herself, how powerless she felt when she was around Ryder. It frightened her, and oddly enough, excited her all at the same time.

"Hi," he said, in that low, husky voice of his. "You look exhausted."

Lynn met his gaze steadily, refusing to allow herself to be sucked into his male charm, and knowing it would do little good to resist. She felt like she was swimming upstream against a raging current, battling for every inch of progress.

"Ryder took us out for Chinese food," Jason announced, plopping himself down on the ottoman in front of his mother. "And then—"

"I want to tell," Michelle cried impatiently. "You already told her about dinner."

"But *I* won the basketball. I should be the one to tell her."

"There was a carnival with rides and everything in the parking lot at the Fred Meyer store," Michelle announced, spitting the words out so fast they fell on top of each other. She ignored her brother's dirty look and continued, "We stopped there and Ryder let us go on all the rides we wanted."

"I won this." Jason held out a furry orange ball, beaming proudly.

"With a little help from Ryder." Michelle's singsong voice prompted the truth.

"Okay, okay, Ryder got down most of the pins, but I knocked some over all by myself."

"Congratulations, son." Lynn couldn't remember the last time Jason had looked so happy. His eyes shone with it and, for the first time in recent memory, he wasn't wearing his army clothes. Lynn didn't know what Ryder had said or done to get him to change, but whatever it was had worked better than anything she'd been able to come up with. A twinge of resentment shot through her, which she stifled. Her thoughts were petty, and she was angry with herself for being so small-minded.

"I got a mirror with Madonna's profile sketched on it," Michelle announced, smugly holding it up for her mother's inspection.

A flash of her own image reflected back at her and caused Lynn to cringe. She looked dreadful—

"Yeah, but you didn't win that." Jason chimed in, interrupting her thoughts. It seemed he wanted to be sure his mother was aware no skill had been involved in obtaining Michelle's mirror.

"Actually Ryder was kind enough to buy it for me," Michelle answered in a disdainfully prim voice meant to put her obnoxious brother firmly in place.

"I want to show Brad my basketball," Jason said, turning his back on his sister. "Can I go over there...it isn't even dark yet."

Oh, the joys of summer, Lynn mused. It was almost nine and almost as light as it had been at three that afternoon.

"Marcy loves Madonna. I want to run over to her house, too, can I?"

Lynn took one look at her children's eager expressions and nodded. Both vanished, leaving Ryder and Lynn alone in their wake. To her dismay, her empty stomach growled and Lynn flattened her hand over her abdomen.

"When was the last time you ate anything?" Ryder asked. His eyes blazed at her as though she'd committed some hideous crime and he was about to arrest her.

Lynn regarded him with a trace of irritation. "Noon. Listen, Ryder, I appreciate you taking the kids for me tonight. It's obvious they had the time of their lives, but I'm a big girl, I can take care of myself. I've even managed to feed myself a time or two."

"Not while working twelve-hour shifts."

"How much time I put in with my own salon is none of your business."

A frown darkened his features and as if to completely discredit her, her stomach growled again, this time loud enough to stir the cat who was sleeping on the back of the sofa.

"Come on," he said, "let's get you some dinner before you pass out."

"I can take care of myself."

"Then do it!"

With quick, efficient movements, Lynn marched into the kitchen and pulled the TV dinner out of the microwave. Whirling around to face him, she yanked open the silverware drawer and jerked out a fork.

"You can't eat that garbage." Ryder contemptuously regarded her meal, wrinkling up his nose as if he found the very smell of it offensive.

"I most certainly *can* eat this . . . just watch me." Before he could argue with her, she stabbed her fork into watery mashed potatoes. They tasted like liquid paper and she nearly gagged, but she managed to swallow the bite and pretend it was nectar from the gods.

"Lynn, stop being so damn stubborn and throw that thing out before it makes you sick." He removed the plastic carton from her hands.

Lynn grabbed it back before he could place it in the garbage. "Stop telling me what to do."

"Okay, I apologize. Now throw that out and cook yourself something decent. You can't work that many hours and treat your body this way."

"Since when have you become an expert on *my* body?" she yelled, growing more furious by the minute.

"Since last night," he yelled back.

Their eyes met in a defiant clash of wills. His were dark and narrowed and hers wide and furious. From the way the grooves at the edges of his mouth whitened, Lynn knew he was having trouble keeping a rein on his temper. For some obscure reason, that bit of insight pleased Lynn. It pleased her so much she had to resist the urge to laugh. He was clearly determined to bend her will to his no matter what it cost. And she was equally determined not to. Most anyone else would have been intimidated by his fierce gaze, but she wasn't. She knew Ryder well—besides, the stakes were far too high.

When he turned away and started sorting through her refrigerator, Lynn laughed out loud. "Just exactly what do you think you're doing?"

He ignored her completely.

Lynn slapped her hands against her sides and groaned. "Good grief, Ryder, don't you see how ridiculous this is? The two of us aren't any better than Michelle and Jason."

He set several items on top of the counter, then started searching through her cupboards until he found a frying pan.

"You're wasting your time," she told him, as he peeled off slices of bacon and placed them in the skillet.

"No, I'm not."

Lynn found the entire episode highly amusing. "If you think I'm going to eat that, you're sadly mistaken."

He didn't rise to her bait.

As if to prove her point, she took another bite of the atrocious TV dinner, choking down a rubbery piece of meat that was floating in something that resembled gravy.

The distinctive odor of frying bacon filled the kitchen, slowly waltzing around Lynn, wafting under her nose and causing her mouth to water. She downed another bite of mashed potatoes, nearly gulping in an effort to force the tasteless mass down her throat.

For all the attention Ryder was giving her, she might as well have been invisible.

"You're wasting your time, Ryder," she told him a second time, angry that he was ignoring her.

He cut a tomato into incredibly thin slices and stacked them in a neat pile. Next he buttered the bread, added just the right amount of salad dressing and then started building the sandwich with thick layers of bacon, lettuce and tomato.

"I'll end up giving that to the cat," she warned.

He folded the bread together, placed the BLT— Lynn's favorite kind of sandwich—on a plate and poured her a tall, cold glass of milk. Next he carried both the glass and the plate to the table and pulled out a chair for her, silently demanding that she sit down and eat.

"I told you it was a waste of time," she said, crossing her arms and purposely directing her nose in the opposite direction.

"Lynn," he coaxed softly, "come and eat."

"No." A lesser woman would have succumbed, but she was beyond reason. More than a silly sandwich was at stake; Ryder was challenging her pride.

Apparently he was prepared for her argument because he marched back to her. He settled his hands on her shoulders and tightened them just a little so she felt his fingers firmly against her flesh, but not painfully. She was conscious of an odd sensation that surged through her blood, an awareness, an exhilaration as if she'd been frozen for years and years and was only now beginning to melt.

"Sit down and eat."

She shook her head.

"Good Lord, you're stubborn."

She gave him a saucy grin, hoping to mock him. She realized her mistake almost immediately—Ryder wasn't a man to be scorned. Harsh lines formed around his mouth and between his eyebrows and fire blazed from his eyes. Lynn had to do something and quick.

"Just who do you think you are?" she flared, attacking him, taking the offense rather than being forced into a defensive position. "You have no right—absolutely none—to tell me what to do."

Ryder's hold tightened on her shoulders and Lynn realized an instant later that she'd made her second tactical error. But this time she was too late to do anything about it.

"I'll tell you what gives me the right," he growled. "This." Before she knew what was happening, his mouth was on hers—his lips hard and compelling and so hot she felt singed all the way to her toes. He took her mouth with a fierceness that claimed her breath. Her eyes were shut tightly and to her further humiliation, low growling sounds rose from the back of her throat that only seemed to encourage him. He sought her breasts, his touch feather light, lingering over each tormented nipple until they throbbed and pleaded for more. Her moaning grew louder, beseeching, and she nearly died with pleasure when he brushed his thumbs over her beaded nipples. A flickering physical pain licked deep at her insides.

Lynn tried to resist him—she honestly tried. Her mind scrambled with a hundred reasons why she should free herself, but it was useless. Beyond impossible. While her head was screaming at her to put an end to this madness, she slid her arms around his neck, clinging to him. She burrowed her fingers through the thick, dark hair at the back of his head, and her tongue darted in and out of his mouth in a game of cat and mouse.

Ryder slid his moist lips from hers to the scented hollow of her neck. Lynn drew in several deep, wobbly breaths in a reckless effort to regain her composure. She had melted so completely in Ryder's arms that he would have to peel her off.

"Lynn."

His harsh intake of breath gave her a little satisfaction. He, too, had apparently been just as affected by their kissing.

"Yes?" Her own voice was low and gravelly.

"Why do you find it so necessary to argue with me?"

"I . . . I don't know."

"You're so hungry you're almost sick with it, and still you won't eat. Why?"

She shook her head, not bothering to mention that she'd cooked the frozen dinner and had every intention of suffering through that—would have, in fact, if he hadn't insisted on cooking her something else. But instead of arguing, she moved her head just a little and opened her mouth against his throat, kissing it. She felt his body tense and smiled, loving the exhilarating sensation of power the action provided her.

"I'm always cranky when I get overly hungry," she explained.

Ryder chuckled, but the sound of his amusement was tainted with chagrin. "Next time, I'll remember that."

Lynn wasn't sure she wanted him to, not when she enjoyed his methods of persuasion so much.

"Will you eat the sandwich now?"

Lynn didn't even have to think about it. "All right."

Ryder released her, and she meekly sat down at the table. She had just taken her first bite when Michelle and Marcy strolled into the kitchen.

"Hi Mom, hi, Ryder." She pulled out a chair, twisted it around and plopped herself down. "Have you told Mom about Wild Waves yet?" The question was directed to Ryder.

He frowned. "Not yet."

"What about Wild Waves?" Lynn inquired, almost afraid to ask. The water park was in the south end of

Seattle and a popular recreation spot. Machine produced waves and huge slides attracted large crowds.

Michelle grinned from ear to ear in a smile that would
dazzle the sun. "Ryder's taking the three of us to the
park Saturday. We're going to take a whole day off and
have fun like a real family, isn't that right?"

Lynn could feel the heat building up in her cheeks.
Not only was Ryder dictating what she ate, but now he
apparently meant to take control of her whole life.

"Michelle," Ryder said, glancing at the girl. "Maybe
it would be best if you gave your mother and me some
time alone."

Ten

Ryder waited until Michelle and her friend had vacated the kitchen. Lynn was irate. Her eyes flashed fire at him, but that was nothing new. She'd been in a foul mood from the moment he walked into the house with the kids. Good Lord, that woman could be stubborn—Ryder hadn't realized how obstinate until just now. Couldn't she see that he was only trying to help her? From the way she was acting, one would assume he'd committed some terrible crime against women's rights. From what the kids had told him, Lynn hadn't had a full day off in months, but apparently suggesting a fun outing was paramount to being a male chauvinist pig. Especially on the heels of their showdown over the sandwich.

All Ryder had wanted Lynn to do was take care of herself, and surely that wasn't so terrible. As for this Wild Waves thing, she needed a day to relax, but from the way her narrowed eyes were spitting fireballs at him, she fully intended to argue with him about this, too.

"What's this about taking Saturday off and going to Wild Waves?" Lynn demanded when he didn't immediately explain.

"I thought it might be a fun thing to do."

"I assumed you were working in a law office and understood minor things like making a living and responsibility? Obviously you think I'm independently wealthy.''

"You know that's not true.'' He tried not to respond in like anger, but to remain coolheaded and reasonable. Apparently the food hadn't had enough time to defuse her ill mood.

"Then you assume that it's no problem for me to flutter in and out of the salon at will? Besides, the lawyers that *I* know work at least six-day weeks.''

"My schedule isn't like that, and you know it.'' For now his workload was light. But it wouldn't always be that way. He wanted to take advantage of the summer months as best he could, using this time to court Lynn and spend time with Michelle and Jason.

"How could I possibly know anything about your schedule?'' she demanded. "You show up at my place at noon, wanting to take me to lunch. Then the next thing I know, you're telling me you have Saturday free to laze away in some park.'' She finished the sandwich, stood and carried the empty sandwich plate to the sink, then turned to face him, her back braced against the kitchen counter. "Well, I can't take time off when I feel like it. Saturday isn't free for me and I have no intention of taking it off—I'm short staffed as it is.''

He shrugged, accepting her decision. There was little else he could do, although his disappointment was keen. "Then don't worry about it. I'll be happy to take the kids myself.''

Her mouth was already open, the argument dying on her lips. "But—''

"Lynn, I thought Wild Waves was something you might enjoy as well.''

"You should never have mentioned my coming in front of the kids. Now they're going to be disappointed."

He mulled that over, then nodded. "You're right." But Michelle and Jason had complained that all their mother ever did was work, suggesting a family outing had slipped out without him giving the matter the proper thought. A day completely free of worry and commitment sounded like just the thing for Lynn. Michelle and Jason both claimed she worked too hard, and Ryder was witness to the fact himself. She was driving herself toward a nervous breakdown, putting in ten- and twelve-hour days, skipping meals, and it didn't look as though she was sleeping well, either.

Ryder longed to wrap her in his arms and protect her. But holding Lynn when she was in this mood was like trying to kiss a porcupine. He could feel her bristle the minute Michelle had innocently mentioned the outing. Kissing her into submission wasn't going to work a second time. In fact, Ryder felt a bit guilty about having used that technique earlier, but she'd angered him so much that holding her had been his only weapon against her stubborn pride. For some obscure reason, he'd managed to convince himself he could control the passion between them. Wrong. The minute her sweet tongue had started teasing him, he'd been on the brink of lifting her into his arms and hauling her up those stairs to make slow, sweet love to her. The only thing that had stopped him was the thought of Michelle and Jason bursting in on them. Thank God he had enough common sense to call matters off when he did.

The time had come to wake up and smell the coffee. When it came to his feelings for Lynn, Ryder was playing with a lit stick of dynamite and the sooner he owned up to the fact, the better. Who the hell did he think he was? Superman? He couldn't kiss her like that and not pay the consequences. Just the memory of the way her silky, soft body had moved against him was enough to make his mouth go dry. He'd waited all these months to claim her as his own, he could wait a little longer. When they *did* make love, and that was inevitable, the timing would be right, and not the result of some heated argument.

"Don't misunderstand me, I'd enjoy a day off," Lynn admitted with some reluctance, "but I just can't."

"I understand that," Ryder returned, although he had trouble accepting it. He walked over to her side and placed his hands on her forearms. She stiffened, which frustrated the hell out of him, and he dropped his arms, not wanting to force another confrontation. The day would come, he assured himself, when she would welcome his touch. For now, she was frightened and confused and in need of a good deal of patience.

"Hi Mom, hi Ryder." Jason stepped into the kitchen, set his basketball on the tabletop and leaned forward. "What's happening?"

"Nothing much," Lynn said and set her plate and glass in the dishwasher.

"You ask Mom about Wild Waves?" The question was directed to Ryder.

"She has to work, son."

Disappointment flashed from his eyes and the smile he'd been wearing folded over into a deeply set frown. "We can still go, can't we?"

"If it's all right with your mother."

"Of course it's all right," Lynn answered eagerly, as though to make up for the fact she wouldn't be there.

Jason nodded, but none of the excitement returned. "We had a good time tonight. Ryder let me go on as many of the rides as I wanted and when that sissy Michelle was afraid to try the hammer, he went with me."

"A man's got to do what a man's got to do," Lynn joked and when she glanced in Ryder's direction, he grinned. "I'm pleased you had such a good time. I hope you remembered to properly thank Ryder."

"Of course I did." Jason pulled out a chair and folded his arms over the top of the stuffed basketball, his look thoughtful. "You took us to Wild Waves once, Mom, don't you remember? But that was when you were home. You used to do a lot of things with Michelle and me before you went to work with those fat ladies... but you don't do much of that anymore."

"I need to make a living, honey."

"I suppose," Jason returned with an elongated sigh. "But sometimes I think we were better off when we were poor."

"Jason," Lynn argued, staring at her son incredulously, as though she couldn't believe her own ears. "That's not true."

She cast Ryder a sideways glance as if she felt it was important for him to believe her. He smiled, telling her that he did.

"I'll be able to take you to Wild Waves another time."

"But when?" Jason cried. "You're always telling me about all the great things we're going to do some day and they never happen."

"Jason, you're being completely unreasonable. Why... look at what we've done this summer."

"What? What have we done this summer, Mom?"

It was apparent that Lynn was searching her memory and was surprised to discover she'd spent far less time with her children than she realized. Her expression became a study in parental guilt. Her energy level was frayed to the edges as it was, and although Ryder had intended to stay out of the discussion, he stepped to Lynn's side and slipped his arm around her shoulder, hoping to lend her his strength. She didn't appreciate the action and he dropped his arm almost immediately.

"The only place we've gone *all* summer is to the precinct picnic," Jason told her righteously.

"I think it's time for bed, Jason, don't you?" Ryder suggested. "You've got a big day at camp tomorrow."

His eyes widened and his grin blossomed, spreading from ear to ear. "Right. Do you want me to tell Marcy it's time to go home, Mom?"

Lynn shook her head. "I'll do that. Now up to bed, young man."

"Okay." He walked over and kissed her cheek, then looked at Ryder and rolled his eyes. "Women expect that kind of thing," he explained, as if it were important for Ryder to understand that he didn't take to kissing girls.

"I know."

With that, Jason traipsed up the stairs and into his room. Lynn stood with her arms folded, staring after her son as though she couldn't quite believe what had just transpired. "He always has an excuse for staying up late. I can't remember the last time he didn't argue with me over bedtime."

With Lynn so exhausted, Ryder realized it was time he left. He didn't want to go, but what he longed for wasn't important right now—Lynn's health was.

"It's time I thought about heading home." He was a bit disappointed when she didn't suggest he stay longer, and mildly annoyed when she didn't so much as walk him to the door. It was all too obvious that she was glad to be rid of him, and that dented his pride. He'd come a long way with Lynn in a short amount of time, but miles of uncharted road stretched before him. At least when he kissed her, he had her attention. That small piece of information helped ease his mind as he climbed inside his car and drove off.

The following afternoon, Lynn sat at her desk, expelled a deep breath and reached for the phone. She couldn't delay calling Ryder any longer. Her finger jabbed out the number of his office as if to punish the phone for making this conversation necessary. Silly as it sounded, Lynn preferred contacting him at Crestron and Powers. It was less personal than calling him at his apartment. She fingered his business card until the honey-voiced secretary came on the line and efficiently announced the name of the firm. Whoever she was, this woman with the peaches-and-cream voice, Lynn didn't like her.

"Could I have Ryder Matthews's office please?"

"May I ask who's calling?"

It was on the tip of Lynn's tongue to demand to know just how many women Ryder had phoning him, but she realized in the nick of time how ridiculous that would have been. That thought alone was enough to prove that she'd made the right decision—she *needed* a day off.

"Lynn Danfort," she answered after a moment. "If he's busy, he can return the call."

"I'll put you through," the woman purred, and Lynn resisted the urge to make a face.

"Lynn, this is a pleasant surprise." Ryder came on the line almost immediately. "What can I do for you?"

Lynn dragged herself away from her thoughts. "Ryder, hello." She felt so foolish now. "It's about Wild Waves on Saturday. I . . . I was wondering if it would be all right if I *did* decide to tag along." There—that hadn't been so bad. Ryder was a gracious man—he'd never given her reason to think otherwise.

"That would be great. I'd love to have you."

"I talked with my assistant, Sharon, and she said that she'd cover for me." Lynn wouldn't mention what else Sharon had said. The woman seemed to think Lynn was a first-class idiot to turn down an outing with Ryder Matthews. *Any* outing, even if it included Michelle and Jason. For her part, including the kids was the only way Lynn would agree to see Ryder. When it came to dealing with her late husband's best friend, she was more confused than ever. She'd thought to avoid him as much as possible. That had been her intention after he'd asked her out that first day at the precinct picnic and then later when he'd come to the salon. She'd refused him both times. But circumstances seemed to keep tossing them together.

Lynn would have liked to blame Ryder for everything that had happened, but she couldn't even salvage her pride with that. And when he'd kissed her, it had been like setting a match to a firecracker, her response was that explosive. Every time Ryder came close to her, Lynn had been left indelibly marked. In the beginning she'd tried to pass her reaction off to the fact she'd been without a man for a long time. She'd dated a bit in the past couple of years, but no one else had been able to elicit the feeling Ryder had—no one except Gary, and that frightened her.

"I'd thought we'd make a full day of it and leave about ten-thirty."

"That sounds fine to me." Sleeping in sounded glorious. "I'll pack us a picnic lunch."

"Bring lots of suntan lotion and plenty of towels."

"Right." Her enthusiasm level increased just talking about the outing. It'd been so long since she'd spent a carefree day lazing in the sun.

"I'm really looking forward to this, Ryder."

He sighed and a wealth of satisfaction hummed through the wire. "Good."

After a few words of farewell, Lynn replaced the telephone receiver, but her hand lingered on the headset. For some obscure reason she couldn't explain or understand, she had the feeling everything was going to change between her and Ryder because of this outing.

Eleven

"Mom, look!"

Lynn and about thirteen other women turned in the direction of the young voice, glancing toward the water where the youngsters were bobbing up and down on the swirling waves. It took Lynn a couple of seconds to realize the boy's voice hadn't belonged to Jason.

The minute the four of them had arrived at Wild Waves, Jason had hit the water like the marines attacking Normandy beach and had yet to come out almost two hours later. Every now and again, Lynn saw him sitting atop his brightly colored tube, riding the swelling waters as if he were master of the universe. To say he loved the waterworks park would be an understatement.

Michelle, on the other hand, had spent an hour fixing her hair before Ryder had arrived. When Lynn had been silly enough to mention that all that mousse would be wasted once she got wet, Michelle had given her a look that suggested Lynn was brain dead. Later Michelle explained that she was styling her hair in case she happened to run into someone she knew. This "someone" was obviously a boy.

"It couldn't be a more perfect day had we planned it," Lynn told Ryder, who was lying back on the blanket, his face turned to the sun, his eyes closed. He'd recently walked out of the pool and his lean muscular length glistened in the bright golden light.

"I *did* plan it," he joked. "I told the person in charge of weather that we needed sun today. One word from me and it was arranged."

"It seems I've underestimated your influence." Her voice was teasing, but she couldn't disguise her pleasure. Ryder had been right; she needed this, far more than she'd been willing to admit. "Do you have anything else arranged that I should know about?"

A slow, easy smile worked its way across his face. "As a matter of fact, I do, but I'm saving that for later." He opened his eyes and looked up at her, his grin devilish and filled with boyish charm. "I suggest you be prepared."

"For what?"

He wiggled his eyebrows up and down several times.

Despite the effort not to, Lynn laughed. It felt so good to throw caution to the wind and leave her worries behind her at least for this one day. She hadn't so much as called Sharon to see how things were going at the salon. If there were problems, she didn't want to know about them. It was amazing how comfortable it felt to bury her head in the sand—or in this case, the water.

"Mom, I'm starved."

This time the voice was unmistakably Jason's. Lynn twisted around and found her son wading out of the deep blue water, his inner tube under one arm and a snorkel in the other.

Lynn straightened and reached for the picnic basket, and small cooler which were loaded with goodies. She brought out a turkey sandwich and a cold can of soda.

Jason fell to his knees and automatically reached for the soda. "Gee, this is fun. Did you see the wave I just took?"

"I...can't say that I did," Lynn admitted. She set out the potato chips and fresh fruit—seedless grapes were Jason's favorite, and she'd packed several large bunches.

"Where's Michelle?" Ryder asked, looking toward the slide area.

"The last time I saw her, she was talking to some guy," Jason told him in a disgruntled voice. "She's hardly been in the water all day. I asked her about it and she got all huffy and told me to get lost. Personally, I think she's afraid of getting her hair wet." He said this with a sigh and a meaningful shrug as if to suggest Lynn arrange intensive counseling for her oldest child. Between bites, Jason added. "I don't think I'll ever understand girls."

"I gave up trying years ago," Ryder admitted.

"Then why do we have anything to do with them?"

Her son was completely serious. "Jason! What a thing to ask."

"*You're* all right, Mom," he was quick to assure her. "It's all the others. Look at Michelle—here we are at the neatest water place in the whole world and she's afraid to go in past her knees because she's afraid someone will splash her hair. It's ridiculous, don't you think?"

"No," Lynn shot back. Michelle was at an age when maintaining her looks was important to her. That was all part of growing up. Within a few years, Jason was sure to experience the same level of conscientiousness. She was sure he wouldn't find it quite so silly then.

"If you'll notice, your mother hasn't spent much time in the water, either," Ryder pointed out. He sat up and shot Lynn a mischievous grin.

"You're worried about your hair, too?" Jason cried as though he couldn't believe his ears. "My own mother!"

"Not exactly."

"Then how come you've only been in the pool a little bit?"

It was more a matter of crowd control. When Lynn first arrived, she'd taken out an inflated raft and had been quickly overpowered by what seemed like several thousand kids, each one eager to ride the waves. All those thrashing bodies had gotten in her way. She simply needed more space.

"Mom?" Jason asked, a second time. "Explain yourself."

Lynn laughed. "There are too many kids out there."

"Too many kids," Jason repeated, stunned.

"I go in and cool off when I get too hot, but other than that I prefer to lie in the sun and perfect my tan."

It looked as though Jason was about to make another derogatory comment referring to her wanting a golden tan. To divert his attention, she took out a package of potato chips and handed them to him. Her tactic worked, and within a minute the boy was too busy wolfing down his lunch to care how much time she spent in the water. As soon as he'd finished eating, he was off again, eager to return to his fun.

Kneeling in front of the picnic basket, Lynn closed the lid and picked up the discarded bits of litter left over from her son's lunch.

"You're getting sun-burned," Ryder commented wryly.

GET 3 BOOKS FREE!

MIRA BOOKS, the brightest star in women's fiction, presents

the *Best* of the *Best*

Superb collector's editions of the very best romance novels by the world's best-known authors!

* **Free Books!** Get one free book by Heather Graham Pozzessere, one by Linda Lael Miller and one by Patricia Potter!

* **Free Gift!** Get a stylish picture frame absolutely free!

* **Best Books!** "The Best of the Best" brings you the best books by the world's hottest romance authors!

GET ALL 3

We'd like to send you three free books to introduce you to "The Best of the Best." Your three books have a combined cover price of $16.50, but they are yours free! We'll even send you a lovely "thank-you" gift—the attractive picture frame shown below. You can't lose!

FREE!

ONLY FOREVER
by Linda Lael Miller
"Sensuality, passion, excitement, and drama ... are Ms. Miller's hallmarks." — *Romantic Times*

FREE!

SWAMP FIRE
by Patricia Potter
"A beguiling love story ..."
— *Romantic Times*

FREE!

SPECIAL FREE GIFT!

We'll send you this lovely picture frame, decorated with celestial designs, absolutely FREE, just for giving "The Best of the Best" a try! Don't miss out—mail the reply card today!

DARK STRANGER
by Heather Graham Pozzessere
"An incredible storyteller!"
— *L.A. Daily News*

©1995 HARLEQUIN ENTERPRISES LTD.

BOOKS FREE!

DETACH AND MAIL CARD TODAY!

THE BEST OF THE BEST™: HERE'S HOW IT WORKS—

Accepting free books places you under no obligation to buy anything. You may keep the books and gift and return the shipping statement marked "cancel." If you do not cancel, about a month later we will send you 3 additional novels and bill you just $3.99 each, plus 25¢ delivery and applicable sales tax, if any.* That's the complete price, and—compared to cover prices of $5.50 each—quite a bargain! You may cancel at any time, but if you choose to continue, every month we'll send you 3 more books, which you may either purchase at the discount price...or return at our expense and cancel your subscription.

*Terms and prices subject to change without notice. Sales tax applicable in N.Y.

If offer card is missing write to: The Best of the Best, 3010 Walden Ave., P.O. Box 1867, Buffalo, NY 14240-1867

BUSINESS REPLY MAIL
FIRST-CLASS MAIL   PERMIT NO 717   BUFFALO, NY

POSTAGE WILL BE PAID BY ADDRESSEE

THE BEST OF THE BEST.
3010 WALDEN AVE.
P.O. BOX 1867
BUFFALO, NY 14240-9952

NO POSTAGE
NECESSARY
IF MAILED
IN THE
UNITED STATES

She paused and glanced down at her arm, but didn't notice any appreciable difference.

"You'd better put on some sunscreen before you get burned." He reached for her hand, lifting her arm as if to examine it. "Let me put it on for you."

"No," she returned automatically. All day she'd taken pains to avoid any type of physical contact with Ryder, even the most innocent of touches. The thought of him sliding his hands up and down her shoulders and over her back was enough to flash huge red warning lights inside her head. This was something to be avoided at any cost.

"Lynn, you're being silly. You aren't used to all this sun."

"I'm fine," she said, fighting the tingling awareness of his fingers holding on to hers. She couldn't allow herself to get too close to Ryder, fearing the power he had to control her body's responses. She tugged at her hand, wanting to free herself before she sought a deeper contact. But Ryder wouldn't release her hand. Instead he lifted it to his mouth and pressed a soft, lingering kiss to its back. His tongue flickered out, moistening the tender skin there. Lynn's heart leaped into her throat at the sensual contact. His eyes, staring at her over her wrist, seemed to convey a thousand words. There were emotions he had yet to verbalize, matters she wasn't prepared to accept. Lynn found herself mesmerized by his dark brown eyes; she couldn't have pulled away had her life depended on it. The world she'd so carefully constructed since Ryder's absence was about to crumple at her feet and yet she dared to linger. Her heart was pounding so hard, she thought it might damage her rib cage.

She managed to pull her gaze from his, dropping it, but to her dismay, she encountered the crisp curling hairs and the hard muscles of his chest. The overwhelming desire to run her fingers through those dark hairs was akin to a physical blow. Ryder's uneven breathing told her he was equally affected by her merest touch. If anything, that increased Lynn's already heightened awareness of him and their situation. With an incredible surge of inner strength, she pulled away and stood abruptly—so abruptly, she nearly stumbled.

"I...think I'll go in the pool for a little bit," she said in a voice that trembled.

Lynn couldn't get away fast enough.

Ryder watched Lynn go with an overpowering sense of frustration. He'd tried being patient with her; he'd taken pains to make this outing as relaxed as possible. From the minute he'd arrived at the house, Ryder recognized that Lynn had carefully chosen to play the role of a good friend. It was obvious that she didn't want to experience the things he made her feel. Apparently she wanted to pretend they'd never kissed, and ignore the fact she'd come to life in his arms. Not once, but twice. It had been difficult, but Ryder had played along, falling into her scheme—for her sake, certainly not because that was the way he wanted it. All along, his intention had been to give Lynn the time she needed to relax and enjoy herself. He didn't want to spoil it by making emotional demands on her. Any kind of demands.

But damn it all, she was driving him crazy. She'd worn a demure one-piece swimsuit, although he was certain she owned more than one bikini. But the modest suit did little to disguise her magnificent body. If anything, it boldly emphasized every luscious curve of her womanly shape. He hadn't thought it was possible to desire her any more than he already did, but watching her move in that swimsuit came damn close to driving him crazy.

Ryder's fingers ached with the need to caress her. When he'd reached for her hand, he felt her involuntary reaction to his touch. She'd shivered slightly and he'd watched, astonished as her nipples went erect. It was as though they were pleading for his hands and mouth to seek them out. The ache in his loins increased with the memory and he drew a deep breath in an effort to minimize his body's response. The problem was she was so damn beautiful, with her wind tousled hair and her sweet face devoid of any makeup. There wasn't a woman alive who could compete with her.

Now, like a frightened rabbit, she was running away from him. His instinct was to reach out and grab her, keep her at his side, demand that she listen to all the love he had stored up in his heart for her. But he couldn't do that, couldn't express all this emotion that burned within his chest. To do so could frighten her into running blindly into the night and if he let that happen, he might never be able to catch her.

Patience, he told himself, repeating the word over and over in his mind.

Lynn's escape into the water had nothing to do with the sun. She'd gone swimming in an effort to cool down from being so close to Ryder. His touch, although light and impersonal, could be compared to falling into a lava bed, Lynn mused. She felt the heat rising in her all the way from the soles of her feet, sweeping through her body like a brushfire out of control. The only thing left for her to do was flee. But the throbbing in her nipples and ache between her legs refused to stop.

There weren't nearly as many kids in the water as there had been earlier. She waded out until she was waist deep and still she didn't feel any of the cooling effect she sought. She went deeper and deeper until she had no choice but to dip her head beneath the water's churning surface. The liquid seemed to sizzle against her red-hot face. Dear God, if only she knew what was happening to her.

She swam underwater until her lungs felt as though they were about to burst. Breaking the surface, she drew in huge gulps of oxygen and brushed the long, wet strands of hair away from her face with both hands.

"Jason would be proud of you." The voice was all too familiar.

"Ryder." She opened her eyes and issued his name on a husky murmur, surprised that he'd been able to find her in the huge pool.

"Lynn, don't keep running from me," his low voice pleaded with her.

Her eyes rounded and she stared at him so long she forgot to breathe. She opened her mouth to deny the fact she was trying to escape, but found she couldn't force the lie.

"Watch out."

Even before the words had completely left his mouth, Lynn was caught in a giant swell of water. Her feet flew out from under her and she was tossed about as easily as a leaf floating in an autumn breeze. A strong pair of hands slipped around her waist and righted her. Led by instinct, she reached out and held on.

Lynn and Ryder broke the surface together, clinging to each other.

"Are you all right?"

"Fine," she said automatically, not pausing to check otherwise.

"I didn't see it coming until the wave was on top of us."

He continued to hold her, bringing her so close to his body that Lynn was amazed the brief span of water between them wasn't boiling and spitting. She'd felt so strongly drawn to Ryder. In that moment, she had as much power to resist him as a stickpin would have against a magnet. Her hands were braced against the sides of his neck and she realized, too late, that she'd reached blindly for him, sensing she would be utterly safe in his arms.

Wordlessly he bent toward her, ever so slightly, and she began to stroke his neck, slipping her hands down the water-slickened muscles of his shoulders, reveling in the strength she sensed beneath her fingertips.

She was unsure of the exact moment it had happened, but a warm, reeling sexual awareness took control of her will, leaving her almost giddy in its wake. Without her knowing exactly how he'd managed to do it, Ryder wrapped his arms fully around her, pressing her to the long, hard length of him. She trembled, fitting snugly into his embrace, powerfully aware of the place where his fingers touched her skin. A tingling sensation spread out from his hands in rippling waves that flooded every cell of her body. Swamped with countless emotions, Lynn didn't know which one to respond to first. Confused, flustered and so completely lost in awareness, she buried her face in the hollow of his neck while she struggled within herself. She drew in several deep, shaking breaths, hoping those would help to clear her head.

While he held her firmly around her waist, he combed her hair away from her face in a slow, soothing action. "I'm never going to leave you again," he whispered. "I couldn't bear it a second time."

Lynn longed to tell him it wasn't his leaving that had confused her so much as his coming back. Her fuddled brain tried to formulate the words, but the thoughts cluttered in her mind. She couldn't think while he continued with his gentle caress. She gasped softly in protest when he slipped his hand from her hair down to her shoulders and back.

She opened her mouth and instantly became aware of his chest hair. The curly, dark hairs had fascinated her earlier and she now realized how close they were to her mouth. Common sense be damned, Lynn decided recklessly, and let her tongue investigate the throbbing hollow of his neck. He tasted like salt and water, pleasant beyond belief. Her mouth opened further, hungrily exploring his skin as if he were a delectable feast, as indeed he was.

"Lynn." Her name was ground out between his teeth.

She ignored the plea in his voice. This was what he wanted, why he'd swum out to find her. It was what she'd longed for all day and had tried desperately to avoid.

She continued pressing kisses up the strong cord of his neck, lapping him with her tongue, sucking and giving him tiny love bites.

He tightened his arms around her. He was moving, carrying her through the water, but Lynn hardly noticed. When she happened to glance up, she noted that he'd found a secluded corner away from the rush of swimmers. She kissed the edge of his mouth to voice her approval. She nipped his earlobe, loving the way his body tensed with the action. He braced his feet farther apart as though expecting an assault.

Lynn gave him one.

She took his earlobe into her mouth, her tongue fluttering in and around, sucking, tasting, nibbling. A sense of hot pleasure flashed through her at the way his pulse exploded against her chest.

He groaned once, softly, and the sound excited her more than anything she'd ever known. He wove his fingers into her hair and she heard his harsh, ragged breath as he gently pulled her away from him. Lynn wasn't given more than a second to catch her breath before he took her mouth with a greed that defied anything she'd ever experienced.

Another wave assaulted them, but Lynn couldn't have cared less and apparently neither did Ryder. They were swept off their feet, tossed and rolled and still they relentlessly clung to each other. When they broke the surface, Ryder helped them back into a standing position. Briefly they broke apart, but he wouldn't allow it for long and kissed her again with a ravenous passion; he seemed to want to devour her whole. Lynn responded with everything that was in her. Her mouth opened to him like the sun coaxing open a flower bud. Their tongues warred, touched and caressed until Lynn thought she would die from pure bliss. He lifted her against his body, holding on to her as if her life were at stake. As her body slipped intimately over his, he groaned anew. The sound inflamed her and she rotated her hips against him, in a movement that was utterly shameless.

"Oh, Lynn."

Her arms were completely around his neck, her fingers digging mindlessly into his tense shoulder muscles. "I know," she cried. "This isn't the time or the place." They were in a public place, although she doubted that anyone had noticed them.

"I want you," he growled into her ear.

She smiled and rubbed her foot down the back of his thigh. "I know... I can feel you."

"Tell me you want me, too. I need to hear it."

What seemed like an eternity passed before she was willing to admit it. Why it should be so difficult to tell him what couldn't be any more obvious was beyond her comprehension.

"Lynn..."

"Yes," she groaned. "Yes, I want you."

He expelled his breath, then leaned his forehead against hers. "I don't dare kiss you," he whispered. "I'm afraid I won't be able to stop."

"I... feel the same way."

"I want to touch you so much. I swear there isn't a place on my whole body that isn't aching. If this is the flu, then it's the worst case I've ever had."

Lynn grinned and lightly brushed her lips over his mouth, needing to touch him, damning the consequences. "I'll have you know, Ryder Matthews, it's not very flattering to be compared to the flu."

"I don't suppose you'd care to being likened to the bubonic plague then, either?"

"That's even worse." Lynn was teasing him, but she was experiencing the same level of frustration. Her nipples had beaded and were throbbing and hard. "Should we get out of the water?" she suggested next, looking for a means of easing this self-inflicted torture.

Ryder grinned and rotated his hips so his arousal became all the more evident. "I don't think we... I dare."

"Do you want to swim?"

"No," he growled. "I want to make love to you."

Having him say it so bluntly had a curious effect upon Lynn. The blood drained out of her face and she felt weak and shaky. Ryder must have noticed because his eyes searched her face, his love-thirsty eyes drinking from her.

"Certainly that doesn't shock you?" he asked gently.

"No," she lowered her gaze and took in a calming breath before explaining. "It's just that . . . it's been a long time for me. I feel like a virgin all over again. I suppose that sounds crazy considering the fact I was married several years and bore two children."

"When it comes to you, I *am* crazy."

Her eyes flew to him. "You are?"

He nodded. "But, Lynn, I already know how very good it's going to be for us."

Lynn did, too. After years of living without a husband, years in which she denied feeling anything sexual, she experienced an awesome passion building within her, like a volcano threatening to explode.

She couldn't keep her hands still. She stroked and caressed his face, loving the feel of his hard jaw, the gentle rasp of his beard and the moist heat of his open mouth. When she couldn't hold back any longer, she nuzzled his throat, licking him with the fever that burned within her.

He kissed her again as though he'd been waiting years and was starving for the taste of her. His tongue alternately caressed and tormented her and Lynn realized his hunger was as ravenous as her own.

"When?" she rasped when his mouth slid from hers. "Ryder, oh, please tell me when." She couldn't believe she was being so forward.

He went still. "When? What do you mean *when*?"

With her hands braced on each side of his jaw, she continued her loving assault. "I want to know how long it will be before we make love. Tonight?" She was shaking so badly that if Ryder hadn't been holding on to her she would have sank to the bottom of the pool. "Oh, no," she groaned, "what about the kids? We're going to have to be so careful." Her lips slid across his cheek and lightly brushed over his lips, darting her tongue in and out of his mouth. "Your place would be better. I think—"

"Lynn..."

"I'm not on the pill, either...I hadn't counted on anything like this...ever. What should we do?"

He tensed. "Why?"

"Oh, Ryder, please, think about it. There are going to be problems with this...minor ones, but we can solve them, I know we can." Once more she angled her mouth over his, feeding him with soft, nibbling kisses, feeding herself, unable to get enough of him. "First of all, I don't think it would be a good idea for Michelle and Jason to know what we're doing. They're young and impressionable and I—"

"Lynn, stop," he interrupted, his voice controlled enough for her to grow still.

Slowly she raised her head. It took her a couple of moments to realize how serious he was. She didn't understand. Some of the excitement and happiness drained from her. "What's wrong?"

"I want to know why you want to make love." he asked her, his gaze never wavering from her face.

"Why?" she repeated, stunned. "Do you always ask a woman that kind of question?" She didn't know what was happening, but whatever it was confused the hell out of her.

"I know what your body is feeling, trust me, love, I feel it, too. All I want you to do is give me one good reason why you're doing this."

"You know the answer to that." She loosened her hold from around his neck and braced her hands against his shoulders, feeling incredibly foolish now.

"I don't know the answer."

"Well . . ."

"Because it feels good?" he offered.

She leaped on that excuse and nodded eagerly. "Yes."

He closed his eyes as though she'd lashed out at him and when he opened them again an emotion she couldn't decipher flickered there.

"That's not enough for me," he told her with heavy reluctance. "I wish to God it was, but it isn't."

"Why isn't it?" she cried. It was enough for her...at least it had been until a few moments ago. She couldn't understand why Ryder was being so unreasonable. One minute he was whispering how much he wanted to make love to her and the next he was making her sound heartless and mercenary.

"I'm not looking for a woman to make me 'feel good.'"

He started to say more, but Lynn wouldn't let him, she dropped her arms and stepped back from him. Water lapped against her breasts and when a large wave came on them, she rode it without a problem.

"If this is a joke, I'm not the least bit amused." Her intention was to sound sarcastic and flippant, but her voice broke. She jerked her chin a notch higher.

"Lynn, please," Ryder whispered, "don't look at me like that."

In response, she twisted away from him, feeling hurt and rejected. Only a minute before she'd come right out and admitted that there hadn't been anyone since Gary. Ryder knew she wasn't...loose, and yet he made her feel callous and coldhearted as if she made this type of arrangement with every man she felt the least bit attracted to.

"I don't know what you want from me," she murmured.

Several moments passed before he answered her, and when he did, his voice was filled with resignation. "No, I don't suppose you do. But you'll figure it out soon enough, and when you do I'll be waiting." That said, he swam away with clean, hard strokes.

Lynn watched him go and noted that he seemed to want to punish the water for what had happened between them.

Exhausted, Ryder continued to pump his arms until the ache in his muscles was stronger than the one in his loins. He was as far away from Lynn as it was possible to get in the crowded swimming area. There wasn't any need to push himself further.

He loved Lynn, wanted her more than he'd ever longed for anything in his life. She'd wanted him, too. Good God, she was on fire for him. He hadn't dared to dream she would feel this strongly for him. But damn it all, he didn't want a physical relationship with her that wasn't rooted in commitment. Her talk about keeping their affair a secret from the kids had been bad enough, but dragging up the subject of birth control was more than he could take. In the blink of an eye, he'd gone from aroused and eager to confused and irritated. He didn't want a casual affair with Lynn. He was looking for more from her than a few stolen moments together to ease the explosive physical need they felt for each other.

He wanted her, all right, but on his own terms. When they made love, there wouldn't be any questions left unanswered, nor would there be any secrets.

Soon enough, she would know what he wanted. Lynn was too smart not to figure it out. Dear God, he prayed, make it sooner because he couldn't take much more of this.

Lynn dried herself off with a thick beach towel, then reached for a light cotton blouse. Her fingers didn't want to cooperate and buttoning it seemed to take a half a lifetime. She was confused and angry and frustrated and excited. Each emotion demanded attention, and in response she ignored them all, making busywork around their picnic site. She folded the towels, and laid out the wet ones to dry, then she picked up a few pieces of litter. When she'd finished, she lay down on her stomach on the blanket and tried to sleep. Naturally that was impossible, but Ryder didn't need to know that. When he returned, she wanted him to think she'd simply forgotten what had happened in the water, and she'd put the entire incident behind her.

She heard him about ten minutes later and forcibly closed her eyes. He reached for a towel, that much she was able to ascertain by the sounds coming from behind her. Then she heard the cooler open and a soda can being opened. That was followed by the unmistakable rustle of him peeling the wrapping off a sandwich.

She frowned, marveling that he was able to overlook what had happened in the pool and sit down and eat. Her stomach was in turmoil and food was the last thing she cared about now.

When she couldn't stand it any longer, Lynn rolled onto her back. Shading her eyes with her hand, she stared up to discover Michelle sitting at the picnic table.

"Hi, Mom. I thought you were asleep."

"Hi," Lynn greeted, feeling chagrined.

"This sure is a lot of fun. I've met some really neat . . . people."

Lynn grinned, knowing exactly which sex these "people" probably were. "I'm glad, sweetie." She hadn't finished speaking when Ryder strolled up and reached for his towel, wiping the water from his face.

"I'm going back to my friends, now," Michelle said and stuffed the rest of her sandwich back inside the wicker basket.

"I'll be back in an hour," Michelle called and was off.

"Bye," Lynn called after her daughter, dreading the confrontation with Ryder more than anything she could remember. So much depended on what he was about to say.

Slowly he dropped the towel away from his face and gazed directly at her. "Are you all right?"

"Sure," she answered with a hysterical little laugh. "Why shouldn't I be?"

Twelve

A week passed and Ryder was amazed at all the ways Lynn invented in order to avoid him. She seemed absolutely determined to forget he existed. It would've been comical if Ryder didn't love her so much and long to put matters right between them. He knew beyond doubt the reason she was doing back flips in an effort to escape him. In the full light of reason, when her head wasn't muddled with passion and need, Lynn was probably thoroughly ashamed of their wanton behavior in the pool. Ryder would have sold his soul to tell her how delighted he'd been by her ready response. Her ripe body had begged for the completion of his. Her kisses had been ravenous, undisciplined and carnal. Every time Ryder thought about the way she blossomed in his arms, he trembled with aftershocks. The memory was like standing too close to an incinerator—he burned with a need she'd created in him.

Ryder cursed himself now for rejecting her offer to make love . . . for refusing himself. But he sought more than the release her body could give him, wanted more than to become Lynn's lover.

He yearned for her heart.

The realization had left him perplexed, and in some ways stunned him. Earlier—before the incident at the water park—he would gladly have accepted what she'd so guilelessly offered him. She didn't love him, he realized, but she would soon enough. Hell, he didn't need the words. He loved her enough for the both of them.

But something powerful and deeply rooted within his conscience had stopped him from making love to Lynn, some sentiment he had yet to name. All he did know was that sleeping with her wouldn't be enough to satisfy him.

If Ryder was bewildered by the extent of his emotional need for Lynn, it was nothing compared to what she seemed to be experiencing. He hungered to talk to her, but when he'd phoned her at the salon and later at the house, she'd asked, both times, that a message be taken and then hadn't bothered to return his calls. He'd tried twice more, but on each occasion, she'd come up with a convenient excuse to avoid talking to him.

He'd gone so far as to stop in at her salon only to be told that she was too busy to see to him then. He was told that if he would be willing to wait a couple of hours, she would try to squeeze him in, but there weren't any guarantees. Frustrated and angry, he'd quickly left.

Next, Ryder phoned Michelle and Jason and took them to a movie, thinking he would surely see Lynn when he dropped them off at the house. But she'd exasperated him once more. When he'd gone to pick them up, Michelle had explained that they needed to be taken to Toni Morris's after the movie. His frustration had reached its peak that night.

Since Lynn seemed to require more time to sort out what was happening between them, Ryder reluctantly decided to give it to her. When she was ready to talk, she would contact him. But there was a limit to his patience and it was fast running out.

* * *

Lynn parked her car outside Toni Morris's house and sat quietly for a couple of minutes, gathering her nerve before talking to her friend. Toni wouldn't let her pussyfoot around the issue, and Lynn knew that. She trusted Toni's insights, and sought her wisdom now.

Lynn's nervous fingers tightened around the steering wheel and she released her breath on a swell of anxiety and defeat.

"Lynn," Toni greeted, when she answered the door. "This is a pleasant surprise. Come in."

Lynn nervously brushed the hair from her forehead. "Have you got a minute? I mean if this is a bad time I could come back later."

Toni laughed. "I was looking for a reason not to mow the lawn. I şhould thank you for stopping by unexpectedly like this. At least I'll have an excuse when Joe gets home."

Lynn made a gallant effort to smile, followed Toni into the kitchen and nodded when the former policewoman motioned toward the coffeepot.

"So how are things developing with Ryder?"

Lynn nearly choked on the hot coffee. Leave it to Toni to cut through the small talk.

"Fine . . . he's been wonderful to the kids."

"I'm talking about *you* and Ryder," Toni pressed.

"Fine," she answered quickly . . . too quickly, calling herself the coward she was.

"I see." The two words were riddled with sarcasm. Toni pulled out the chair opposite Lynn and sat down. The air seemed to crackle with tension until Toni added, "How much longer are you planning to avoid him?"

Lynn's jaw flopped open. "How'd . . . you know?"

Toni's answering smile was fleeting. "Michelle made some comment about not knowing why Ryder had to drop the two of them off at my place when you were supposed to be home. And frankly, you didn't do a good job of avoiding me that night, either."

"Why is it everything I do is so transparent?" Lynn asked, throwing her hands into the air. She felt like a witless adolescent.

"It's not as bad as you think," Toni answered with a saucy grin. "I know you, that's all." Toni took a couple of seconds to stir sugar into her coffee. "When was the last time you saw Ryder?"

"It's been over two weeks now."

"Did you argue?"

Lynn dropped her gaze so fast, she feared she'd strained her neck muscles. "In...a manner of speaking. He tried to call me several times, and stopped by the salon once, but I...I was busy."

Toni snickered softly at that bit of information. "When was the last time you heard from him?"

"Nine days ago."

"And you're ready to talk?"

Lynn nodded. She'd been ready for almost a week, but Ryder hadn't contacted her. It was as if he'd dropped off the face of the earth. The first few days after their outing, she would have preferred death to confronting Ryder. Now she felt lost and terribly lonely without his friendship. Noise violated her from every direction, but the silence was killing her. In the past week, Lynn had been short-tempered with the kids, restless and uneasy at work. It was as though she'd walked into a giant void. Nothing felt right anymore. Nothing felt good.

"He's waiting for you to come to him."

The thought immobilized Lynn. She froze, the coffee cup raised halfway to her mouth. It was one thing to be willing to talk to Ryder, but to contact him herself demanded a special kind of courage. If she knew what to say, and how to say it, it would help matters considerably, but all she could think about was how much heat there'd been in the way she'd kissed him and pleaded with him to make love to her.

Just the memory of that afternoon was enough to raise her body's temperature by several degrees. She'd practically begged Ryder to make love to her. She'd thought that was what he'd wanted, too, but then he'd told her that wasn't enough. The way he'd acted led her to believe she'd insulted him. She couldn't understand that, either. Ryder had admitted he wanted her, and yet he'd been totally unreasonable. When she'd brought up Michelle and Jason and the need for some form of birth control, he'd backed away as if she'd slapped him.

"Well?" Toni demanded.

"You think I should be the one to call him?"

"That's what you came here for me to tell you isn't it?"

"I...I don't know." She set down the mug and wiped a hand over her face, feeling tense and ill at ease. "Ryder makes me feel again and, Toni, that frightens me. Just thinking about him causes me to get all nervous and hyper. I wish he'd never come back and, in the same moment, I thank God he did. I'm so scared."

"Why?"

"If I knew that I wouldn't be sitting here with my knees knocking," Lynn cried, irritated by the way her friend continued to toss questions at her. "I don't like the way I feel around Ryder. I was comfortable the way things were before."

"You were miserable."

"I wasn't."

Toni's responding grin was off center. "That's not the story I got the day of the precinct picnic. You told me how you weren't sleeping well and how restless you'd become over the past several months."

Lynn tried to argue, but knew it was useless. Toni was right. Leaning back in her chair, her friend reached for the telephone receiver on the kitchen wall and handed it to Lynn. "Go ahead. I'll conveniently disappear and you can talk to your heart's content.

"But—"

"I hear the lawn calling to me now," Toni joked. She braced her hands against the table's edge and scooted back her seat. "I'm out of here."

"Toni, please, I don't know what to say."

"You'll think of something."

As it turned out, Lynn didn't need to come up with anything brilliant to start the conversation. Ryder was out of the office and when she tried his apartment, she got his answering machine. She left a message on it, hating the way her voice wavered and pitched when she was trying so hard to sound cheerful and happy as though she'd contacted him every day of the week. God only knew what Ryder would think when he listened to it. Given the chance she would have gladly called back and erased the message, but it wasn't possible.

Toni glanced up expectantly and turned off the mower when Lynn came out of the house.

"He wasn't at the office or at his apartment," Lynn explained. "I . . . left a message on his machine so stop looking at me like I'm some kind of coward."

"If the shoe fits, my friend . . ." Toni laughed.

* * *

It was almost midnight and Ryder still hadn't returned her call. Hours before Lynn had given up expecting to hear from him. She was getting a taste of her own medicine and the flavor was definitely bitter. Depression settled over her shoulders like a heavy homemade quilt. Ryder was through with her and she had no one to blame but herself.

Forcing her attention away from the clock, Lynn focused on the ledger that was spread across the kitchen table. She tightened her fingers around the pencil until it threatened to snap in half. She'd gone over these figures so many times that the numbers had started to bleed together. No matter how many different ways she tried, nothing added up the way it should. Maintaining her own books for Slender, Too shouldn't be this complicated. She'd taken bookkeeping in high school and was familiar with the double-entry system, and yet . . . like everything else this summer, nothing was working out the way she planned.

Okay, so she'd blown it with Ryder. The disappointment was keen, but she'd suffered through disappointment before. It hurt, but it wasn't fatal. In many ways she was grateful to him. He'd waltzed into her life at a critical moment. She'd worked so hard in the past three years, seeking contentment in her children and her job, paying the price and never questioning the cost. In a few short weeks, Ryder had done something no other man had been able to do in a long time. He'd awakened her to the fact that she was a woman—a warm, generous woman made to feel and love. Since Gary's death, she'd done everything within her power to ignore that part of herself.

The sound of the front door opening caught her by surprise. Lynn leaped to her feet and met Ryder in the entryway. The sight of him bolted her to the floor.

"I would have knocked, but I didn't think you'd open the door once you saw it was me," he accused her, his voice filled with cynicism.

"That's not true—" She glanced up the stairs, grateful that Michelle and Jason were sound asleep.

"The hell it isn't," he shouted. "You've done everything you could to avoid me in the past two weeks and I'm fed up with it."

"There's no reason to shout." He'd been drinking, but he wasn't anywhere close to being drunk. He knew exactly what he was saying and doing, but that didn't reassure her any.

"I happen to feel there is. How much longer do you plan to bury your head in the sand?"

"If you think you can stand here and insult me, then let me assure you, you'd be doing us both a favor if you left."

"You can forget that."

Lynn refused to answer him. She whirled around and returned to the kitchen. She seated herself at the table and reached for the calculator. To her dismay, Ryder followed her inside.

He stood there silently for several moments, then twisted the ledger around and ran his gaze down the pale green sheet. "What's this?"

"The books for the salon. Not that it's any of your business."

"It's almost midnight."

"I'm well aware of the time, thank you," Lynn answered primly.

"Why are you working on those?"

She couldn't very well admit that she hadn't been able to sleep... hadn't even tried because she was mooning over her relationship with him. Working on balancing her books helped keep her mind off how she'd messed everything up between them.

"I'm not leaving until you answer me," Ryder demanded.

"I enjoy doing my own books."

He sniggered at that. "Sure you do. It's midnight."

"I... couldn't sleep."

"Why not?"

"That's none of your business." At all costs, she avoided looking in his direction.

"You don't need to answer that," he told her crisply. "I already know. You were thinking about me, weren't you? Regretting our day together and how you'd moved your body over mine in the water. You're wishing now you hadn't been so blatant in your wants. You're thinking that maybe I would have made love to you if you'd been a little more subtle."

His arrogance nettled her beyond belief. "Of all the nerve! You're vulgar, Ryder."

"Do you honestly believe I didn't know how much you wanted me?"

"Stop it," she cried, feeling her cheeks fill with flaming color.

"Honey, you wanted me so badly you practically burned me alive. I'm still smoldering two weeks later."

A husky denial burned on her lips. She *had* wanted him, but she would never admit it. Not now, when he was throwing the matter in her face, forcing her to deal with her body's response to him. Lynn preferred to forget the entire incident and go on with their relationship as though nothing had happened. But from the way he was looking at her, she realized the likelihood of that happening was slim.

Ryder turned her around, secured her jaw with one hand and lowered his mouth to hers.

Lynn struggled, but all her efforts only succeeded in exhausting her strength. When flinging her arms against his hard chest, and arching her back didn't help, she pressed her lips firmly together. Even that did little good. Ryder used his tongue as an instrument of exquisite torture. It flicked softly over her lips, coaxing them open and when she relaxed ever so slightly, he outlined the shape of her lips until her moans of anger and outrage became soft gasps of bliss. Finally, without any force from him, her mouth parted, welcoming the intrusion of his tongue.

"That's the way, Lynn," he praised her. "Enjoy it, love, enjoy it. Be honest, to yourself and to me."

His words were all the encouragement she needed. She folded her arms around his neck and without her being certain how he managed it, he lifted her from the chair and seated himself, setting her in his lap.

He broke off the kiss and his breath was warm and moist as it drifted over her upturned face. He smelled of expensive whiskey and she realized that was what she'd been tasting and loving. He didn't need to apply any pressure for her to welcome him a second time. He thrust his tongue deep into her mouth and she moaned anew at the correlating stab of desire that shot through the most intimate parts of her femininity.

His breathing was as rapid and as unsteady as her own when Ryder finished. With his gaze holding hers, he worked at the buttons of her shirt. His fingers were trembling. "You wanted this the other day, too, and I wanted to give it to you."

Too late, Lynn realized his intent. "Ryder, please don't," she begged. "I don't like it when you touch me. We shouldn't be doing this—"

He ignored her small cry of protest, obviously recognizing her lie, and pushed the shirt from her shoulders. Before she knew how he could work so quickly, he'd unfastened the front clasp of her bra. The air felt cold and harsh against her exposed breasts. He groaned out loud, then cupped their undersides and bunched them together. His thumb whisked across the sensitive tops. Lynn gasped and bit into her bottom lip. Her intention had been to tell him to stop, to deny the incredible sensations that washed over her like a tidal wave. He wanted her to own up to her feelings, and still she held back, furious with him for forcing her to confront her feelings and even more furious with herself for wanting him so much.

"You wanted me to do this the other day, didn't you?" he whispered, coaxing the truth from her.

Lynn refused to answer him.

He punished her by fanning her extended nipples with his thumb until they ached and throbbed. "Didn't you?" he demanded a second time.

"No," she lied, denying him the satisfaction of the truth.

His eyes filled with disappointment, but he wouldn't be denied and it showed in the look he gave her. "Somehow, I don't believe you."

It wasn't until he spoke and his moist breath settled over her beaded nipples that she realized his intent. She made a loud murmur of protest, but that quickly turned to a sigh of exquisite pleasure at the touch of his warm, wet tongue against her breast. He licked and despite herself, Lynn whimpered.

"You want something more now too, don't you?" he asked her softly, then added, "I'll give it to you, Lynn, all you have to do is be honest with me."

She would die before she would tell him what she was feeling.

He must have seen the determination in her eyes because he laughed softly and tormented her until she was squirming and tossing her head from side to side.

"Please," she begged, when she couldn't bear it any longer.

"Please what?"

In response, Ryder took her nipple between his lips and held it there, breathing his satin warmth on it until Lynn thought she would die.

"Ask me, Lynn." His own voice contained a thread of pleading.

He tugged on her gently, and flicked his tongue over the hardened nipple. He slid his hand up the inside of her thigh, stopping just short of the apex of her jeans. Her body was pulsing with a need so great it surpassed desire. He moved his hand higher, and she whispered his name.

"That's not what I want to hear. Do you want me, Lynn? Do you?"

"Yes, Ryder, oh please." A sob tore through her throat while he poised his mouth over her nipple. "Suck me," she whimpered. "Oh . . . please."

With a cry of utter contentment he fit his mouth over her breast with a hunger and need that had driven them both to the edge of sanity. He tugged at her gently, until her moans became lost in her dizzying desire.

Thirteen

Somehow Ryder was able to move away from Lynn. He walked over to the kitchen sink, braced his hot hands against the cool ledge and closed his eyes to the torment that racked him. He hadn't wanted to push her like that, but he needed to force her to take responsibility for her own desires. She was so damn good at avoiding her feelings. Every cell of his own body demanded release, every fiber of his being sought completion with her, but he couldn't allow himself to give in to his baser instincts. Not like this. Not now.

He'd been a fool to come to her this way. An angry fool. His actions may have caused him to lose the only woman he'd ever loved. Ever would love.

"Are you angry with me again?" Lynn asked, in a voice that trembled with distress.

Her soft pleading stabbed through his soul. Slowly he turned to face Lynn. "No."

She'd fastened her blouse, but her eyes were filled with despair and longing. Ryder tightened his hands into fists of resolve. "I shouldn't have come here tonight. If anyone deserves an apology, it's you. I had no right to say and do those things to you."

Slowly Lynn lowered her gaze. "You were right about me not being able to sleep because I was thinking of you. I spent half the night hoping you'd answer my call.''

"Answer your call?"

Her face shot upward. "You mean you didn't get my message? I left one on your machine.''

Defeated, Ryder rubbed a hand across his weary face. All this hopelessness, this overwhelming sense of frustration could have been eliminated if he'd gone home when he was finished at the office the way he should have. Instead he'd walked along the Seattle waterfront, depressed and discouraged. Later he'd sat in some uptown bar and found courage at the bottom of a bottle. He felt sick with himself now. He'd come to Lynn for all the wrong reasons, intent on forcing her to accept her feelings for him—whatever they were.

Frustration filled his mouth. He couldn't look at her, didn't dare for fear of what he would see in her eyes. The only thing left to do was leave, and pray she would find it in her heart to forgive him.

He started for the front door when she called him.

"Ryder?"

He stopped, as though waiting for her instructions. He felt completely at her mercy. If she were to tell him to stay out of her life, he would have no recourse but to do as she asked. His intent had been to crush her, to bend her to his will. His higher intentions couldn't overcome his actions. Dear God, when he remembered the way he'd tormented her, there could be no forgiveness. None.

He heard the sound of her chair as she stood. Still he didn't move, couldn't have even if the fate of the entire world rested on his actions.

She placed a hand on his elbow, then abruptly dropped it. "I was wondering . . ." Her voice was little more than a whisper. "I know it's probably more than what you want, but..."

"Yes," he coaxed, almost afraid to hope.

"Would it be all right, if the two of us...you and me started dating?"

Ryder turned, his heart ready to burst with the generosity of the second chance she was offering him. For a long moment, all they did was stare at each other. Lynn was the first to look away.

His sigh of relief had a wounded quality. When he'd kissed and held her, his actions hadn't been completely prompted by love and concern the way he'd wanted to believe—the way she deserved. He'd trampled on her heart, dealing her emotions a crippling blow and all in the name of his stupid pride. "I should never have come," he told her, his face dark with self-anger.

"I'm glad you did."

"You're glad?" He couldn't believe what he was hearing.

"I'm such a coward, Ryder, in so many ways."

Lynn a coward! She was possibly the most fearless woman he'd ever known. "No, honey, that's not true. I've been pushing you too hard and it hasn't worked. I just don't know what to do anymore."

She raised her gaze to his and looked straight at him. Her eyes were wide and filled with incredible longing. Ryder felt his knees weaken. If he were to press the issue, they would probably end up making love before the night was over. God knew, it was what they both wanted.

"I think dating is a great idea," he said. "We'll get reacquainted with each other the way other couples do." His words were more abrupt than he'd intended, but he had to turn his thoughts around before he and Lynn landed in bed and wondered how they'd gotten there so soon.

Lynn nodded.

"Can you go out with me tomorrow night? Dinner? Dancing? Anything you want."

"Dinner would be fine."

Her smile trembled on her lips and it took everything within him not to lean down and taste her once more. Briefly he wondered if a lifetime of her special brand of kisses would ever be enough to satisfy him. Somehow he doubted it.

"Do you want some coffee before you leave?"

Her offer surprised him and his look must have said as much.

"There's a pot already made," she explained. "I don't think it would be a good idea for you to drive when you've been drinking."

His actions had been sobering enough, but he couldn't refuse the excuse to be with her longer. "I'll take a cup—thanks for the offer."

She seemed almost glad as she moved out of the entry and back inside the kitchen. He joined her there and watched as she brought down two ceramic mugs and filled them both.

Ryder sat at the table and his gaze fell upon the ledger. He frowned once more. "Are you having problems?"

She nodded, sitting across from him. "Something's off. I can't get this sheet to balance for the life of me."

"Put it away," he suggested. "The mistake will be easier to find in the morning."

"That's what I thought yesterday."

For a long moment, Ryder resisted asking her, but he couldn't bear not knowing. "How long have you been struggling over this?"

"A week now," she admitted with some reluctance.

"Do you always do your own books?"

"I have from the beginning." A sense of pride lit up her eyes. "I like to keep my hands on every aspect of my business. It means a great deal to me."

"I don't suppose you've ever thought of hiring an accountant to balance your books," he made the suggestion lightly, although it troubled him to have Lynn drive herself to the edge, complicating her life with details others could handle far more efficiently.

"No."

Her answer was hot and automatic. He was treading on thin ice, and knew it, but still he couldn't keep himself from stepping out further. Lynn was stretching her endurance—there wasn't any need to push herself this way. He was doing them both a disservice to stand by and say nothing.

"A good accountant would save you countless hours of frustration."

"I prefer to do my own books, thank you. Besides, hiring a bookkeeper would be much too expensive."

Ryder bit his tongue to keep from telling her that she should at least check it out. She was wasting needless energy when an accountant could balance her books within a couple of hours, in addition to advising her about local and federal taxes, plus payroll.

"Slender, Too, is mine, Ryder. I handle my business affairs the way I want."

He raised both of his hands in surrender, backing off. It bothered him that Lynn was so prickly about taking his advice. He was only looking to help her, but it was obvious she didn't want him butting into her business. In the years since he'd been away, Lynn had gained a fierce independence and seemed to want to prove how capable she was at doing everything on her own. He didn't doubt that, but he fervently wished she were more open to suggestions.

Ryder gulped down the coffee. "What time tomorrow?"

"Is seven too early?"

"That's fine."

He stood, and when he did, Lynn joined him. She walked him to the front door and stepped into his arms as though she'd been doing it half her life. He kissed her goodbye, making sure the kiss would last him until the following night.

"Hi, Mom." Michelle bounced herself down on top of the queen-size mattress in the master bedroom where Lynn was dressing. "So you're going out to dinner with Ryder?"

Methodically, Lynn finished fastening the tiny pearl buttons to her blue silk blouse. "I already told you that."

"Yeah, I know."

"Then why the comment now?" Lynn knew she was being defensive, but she couldn't help it. All day she'd been looking forward to this evening with Ryder and at the same time dreading it. They couldn't seem to be in the same room together without a type of spontaneous combustion exploding between them. "I thought you liked Ryder."

"I love him. He's been great. This summer would have been a real drag without him."

Lynn wasn't convinced she could accept that. "But you're not sure how you feel about the two of us going out . . . is that it?"

"I know how *I* feel and so does Jason. In fact, the two of us were talking and we decided—"

"What?" Lynn asked when her daughter stopped abruptly.

Michelle looked mildly shaken. "Never mind."

"Michelle, I want to know what you and your brother were talking about, especially if it concerns me and Ryder."

"It's nothing. Really."

"Michelle," her voice lowered to a threatening cadence.

"Mom, I'm sorry, I can't tell you. Jason and I made a pact. I didn't want to go as far as to swear on my own life, but you know Jason. He's into this Rambo stuff so thick that he didn't give me any choice but to do what he said military style. Did you know commandos force their men to sign everything in fresh blood?"

Lynn managed to swallow a smile. "Did he make you do that?"

"He wanted to, but I refused. But he *did* manage to swear me to secrecy . . . so I can't say a word of what we talked about and decided."

"I understand."

Michelle heaved a giant sigh. "I will tell you this much, though," she admitted in a soft whisper. "Both Jason and I are real glad that you're going out to dinner with Ryder, even if it does mean we have to have a baby-sitter—which is completely unnecessary, you know?"

Lynn didn't. "The baby-sitter is for Jason's benefit, but don't tell him that, okay?"

"Okay," Michelle agreed, placated.

"And I'm pleased to hear you don't object to my going out with Ryder."

"Actually it isn't any real surprise after the day at Wild Waves."

Heat suffused Lynn's face until she was sure her color would rival a peeled beet's. It would have been too much to hope Michelle and Jason didn't notice the electricity between her and Ryder that afternoon.

The doorbell sounded from downstairs.

"I'll get it," Michelle cried, flying off the bed. "I think it must be Ryder."

Lynn knew it had to be. With her daughter gone, she took a couple of extra moments to check her appearance in the mirror. Only partially satisfied, she flattened her hands down the soft pleats of her plaid skirt. Her heart was ramming against her ribs in anticipation. Ryder hadn't said where they would be dining and she prayed she'd dressed appropriately.

He was waiting for her at the bottom of the stairs, and when she started down the staircase, his eyes went directly to her. Dressed carefully in a stylish suit and tie, he'd never looked more handsome.

"Lynn." He made her name a caress. "You look lovely."

"Thank you." Lynn noticed the way Michelle poked her younger brother with her elbow. The two children looked at each other and nodded approvingly.

"Don't worry about coming home early," Michelle told Ryder excitedly. "Jason and I are watching videos and then going to bed early. Isn't that right, Jason?"

"Right." He offered Ryder a crisp military salute. "Sir," he added in afterthought.

A smile crowded Ryder's mouth and the edges of his lips quivered slightly. "At ease."

Jason dropped his arm and nodded. "Be sure to stay out as long as you want. Michelle and I want you to... there's no need to hurry home on our account."

While Ryder talked to her two kids, Lynn moved into the kitchen and gave a few instructions to the sitter. Ryder joined Lynn a couple of moments later with the phone number to the restaurant where they would be dining.

After a few choice instructions to the kids, Lynn reached for her purse and a light sweater. Ryder's hand, at the small of her back, directed her to his car, which was parked in front of the house. He held open the passenger door for her, and directed his gaze to her mouth. She thought he might want to kiss her and was mildly disappointed when he didn't. It wasn't until Lynn snapped her seat belt into place and she noticed Michelle and Jason studying her from the living-room window, that she understood Ryder's hesitancy.

They traveled the first five minutes in silence. "I've been thinking about you all day," Lynn spoke first, wishing she didn't feel like such a dunce in Ryder's company.

"I can't remember when I've looked forward to an evening more," he answered. He reached for her hand, raised it to his lips and kissed her fingertips.

The simple kiss went through her like an electric shock. Lynn sucked in her breath and bit into the soft flesh of her inner cheek. Her nipples pearled and she prayed he didn't notice.

He did, but the knowledge appeared to please him. He entered the freeway and headed south toward Tacoma. "There's a new seafood restaurant someone was telling me about. I thought we'd try it."

Lynn folded her fingers around the strap of her purse, which rested in her lap. "I suppose you remember how much I love lobster."

"This place is said to serve huge portions."

Lynn couldn't help smiling. She remembered once when the three of them had gone out for dinner and she'd ordered lobster, but when her meal arrived, she'd been outraged at how tiny her serving had been. Disappointed, Lynn had muttered that it should be illegal to kill anything that small.

"We had so many good times, didn't we?" she asked casually.

Ryder nodded, but she noted that he didn't embellish on any memories. She didn't blame Ryder, because talking about the good times with Gary would put a damper on their evening. They'd both loved him so much and nothing could be said that would wipe out the past.

"I had a busy day today," she tried next.

"Oh? Did another of your employees phone in sick?"

"No...I took time off this afternoon to call an accountant."

Ryder's gaze flew from the roadway to Lynn.

"Don't get excited," she said, "my attitude was rotten. The only reason I contacted him was to prove how wrong you were. I knew an accountant would cost me an arm and a leg and I couldn't possibly afford one."

"And?"

"And...he actually sounded quite reasonable so I took everything in to him and we talked. What takes me two days to accomplish, he can do in about twenty minutes. Everything's done by computer these days. I wasn't keen on having him keep my books overnight ... I'm always needing to write a check for one reason or another, but he doesn't need it. He makes copies of my ledger pages, assigned each account a number so that all I need do is write that figure on each check. It's so simple I could hardly believe it.''

"Expensive?"

"Not at all. I should have done this in the beginning. He's helping me with my quarterly taxes, too, and with other things I didn't even know that I should be doing." She expelled a deep sigh when she finished.

"That wasn't so hard was it?"

"What?"

"Telling me you hired an accountant."

"No, it wasn't. You were right, Ryder, and I'm grateful you said something, although I'm sure my attitude last night didn't make it easy."

If he longed to remind her how difficult she had made it, he didn't, and Lynn was pleased. Ryder was a rare kind of man. More rare than she'd realized.

The restaurant was situated on Commencement Bay and they were seated by the window, which offered a spectacular view of the water. Sailboats with their boldly hued spinnakers floated past, adding dashes of bright color to the evening horizon. After their shaky beginning, Lynn was surprised at how easily they fell into conversation. Ryder told her about an important case he'd been assigned, listing the details for her. As they were talking, Lynn noticed several women glancing toward them, their looks envious. She couldn't blame them, Ryder was incredibly handsome.

By the time they were served their dinner a band had started to play in the background. The music seemed to wrap itself around Lynn like a steel cable. She set her fork aside and briefly closed her eyes.

"I remember how much you like to dance."

"And I remember how much you don't."

His grin was filled with wry humor. "Right now, I'd use any excuse to hold you."

She lowered her gaze. "Oh, Ryder, don't say things like that."

"Why not?"

Lynn lowered her eyes. She didn't know how to tell him that it wasn't necessary. He didn't need to invent a reason to take her in his arms. She would go there willingly, happily. All he ever had to do was ask.

When the waiter carried away their plates, Ryder stood and offered her his hand. Lynn accepted it and when they reached the edges of the crowded dance floor, she felt as though she floated into his embrace. Ryder wrapped one arm around her waist and Lynn tucked the side of her head against his jaw, cherishing the feel of his hands, which were so gently securing her to him. She rarely danced anymore—and yet it was as though she'd been partners with Ryder all her life. She fit into his arms as if she'd been handpicked for the position.

"You feel good against me," Ryder whispered close to her ear, and the tremble in his voice said far more than his words.

Lynn closed her eyes and nodded. He felt incredibly good, too. Warm, vital, alive and male...so very male. The music whirled around her like an early morning mist, touching her, caressing her soul with velvet.

The song ended and reluctantly, Lynn dropped her arms. "Thank you, Ryder." She started to move away, appreciating the generosity of him dancing with her once, but he caught her hand, stopping her.

"If you're willing to risk me stepping on your toes a second time, I'm game for another song."

She smiled up at him shyly and nodded. The music hadn't even started when she reached up and folded her arms around his neck.

"The last time you held me like this, we were in the water," Ryder whispered against her hair, his breath heavy. "It was torture then, too." He moved ever so slightly and she followed his lead. Her thighs slid intimately against his. Although her skirt and his pants barred her from experiencing the smooth satiny feel of their bare legs rubbing together, it didn't seem to matter—the sensation was there.

Ryder tightened his grip around her waist, pressing her stomach provocatively against his own. Her breasts were flattened over his torso and her nipples throbbed with the seductive movements of the impossibly slow dance.

"Lynn," he whispered her name in soft agony. "Either we get off this floor now or we're doomed to spend the rest of the night here."

The outline of his hardness moved against her lower abdomen and she sighed, feeling a wild sensation of power. "Let's leave."

"In a minute," he groaned, taking in several deep breaths.

Once outside, the evening air felt cool against her flushed cheeks. "I could have danced all night," she said with a meaningful sigh, chancing a look in his direction. Almost from the moment they'd stepped on the dance floor, it had been apparent that Ryder was distinctly uncomfortable holding her that intimately in such a public place.

Ryder groaned at her light teasing and shook his head. "You're a wicked woman, Lynn Danfort."

She grinned. "Nice of you to say so."

The ride back to Seattle was accomplished in companionable silence. Ryder held her hand as though he needed to feel her close. Lynn experienced the same need, and at the same time she found it essential to root herself in reality.

Ryder exited off the freeway, but instead of heading in the direction of her house, he pulled onto a side street, turned off the engine and braced both hands against the steering wheel.

"What's wrong?"

Ryder expelled his breath forcefully. "I don't know where to go."

Lynn frowned. "I don't understand."

"If I take you back to your place, Michelle and Jason will be all over us."

"Yes," she agreed, "they will."

"But if I take you to my apartment we're going to end up making love. There won't be any way either of us is going to be able to stop." He paused and looked at her, studying her as if expecting her to deny the obvious. "I'm right, aren't I?"

Lynn nearly swallowed her tongue, seeking a way to deny the truth, but she couldn't meet his gaze and lie. "Yes," she admitted in a choked whisper.

Silence seemed to throb between them.

"I'm ready to explode anytime I get near you." Inhaling a slow, silent sigh, Ryder reached for her, taking her by the shoulders. He stared at her for a long moment, then cupped her chin in one hand and tilted back her head as he pressed his mouth over hers. His tongue nudged her lips apart and slipped inside her mouth. Lynn was convinced he only meant to sample her lips, but the instant she opened her mouth to him, Ryder lost control. His kiss was filled with hunger, passion and heat...such unbelievable heat. If a man could make love with his mouth, Ryder did so with that one kiss.

They broke apart, breathless. Feeling spineless, Lynn slumped against him and laid her cheek on his chest. No kiss had ever affected her more and she wondered if Ryder felt anything close to what she was experiencing.

His hand gently cupped her breast. Lynn sighed and leaned toward him, unconsciously seeking more. Ryder rewarded her with a gratifying sound and flicked his thumb over her aroused nipple.

"See what I mean," he whispered.

She nodded.

Ryder kissed her again, although she was sure he hadn't wanted to... at least not there on the dark street with cars buzzing past them.

Lynn laced her fingers through his hair, exalting in the feel of his mouth loving hers. He broke off the kiss and pressed his forehead against hers, taking in huge breaths as though to gain control of his needs.

Lynn felt as though she were about to incinerate. Ryder could do all this to her with a single kiss. God only knew what would happen if they were to go to bed together. She trembled at the thought.

"Are you cold?" Ryder asked, rubbing his hands up and down the length of her arms.

"No. I'm burning up."

"Me, too. Sitting anywhere close to you I come away scorched."

"I'm sorry," she breathed.

"I'm not."

"You're not?"

"No, it tells me how good it's going to be for us."

Lynn frowned, not knowing how to comment. Ryder utterly confused her. They couldn't get close to each other without threatening to ignite anything within a half-mile radius. And yet whenever the subject of making love came up, Ryder tensed and withdrew from her.

"We can't go on like this." He moved his hands over her throat and chest, stroking her breasts. Everywhere his fingers grazed her, Lynn tingled.

"What are we going to do?" she asked, on a husky whisper, hardly able to speak.

"The only thing we can." Once more he lightly brushed her nipples. They didn't need anything more to bring them to an aching hardness.

Whatever he suggested had to be better than this agony. She was about to melt at his feet.

"You aren't going to like it," he said, straightening, his look serious.

"What?"

"I think we should get married. The sooner the better."

Fourteen

"Married," Lynn echoed, stunned. "Married?"

He looked past her, refusing to meet her startled gaze. "I know this must come as something of a surprise. I didn't mean to blurt it out like this, but honestly, Lynn, I don't see any other way around it."

"I—"

"I love you. I love Michelle and Jason and they love me. I want the four of us to be a family...a real family. At night, when I crawl into bed, I want you at my side to love me and ease this ache of loneliness. When I'm old and gray, there's no one I'd rather have at my side."

"Oh, Ryder..." Her voice trailed off and she lowered her eyes. He was offering her the sun and the moon. Huge salty tears formed in the corners of her eyes.

He kissed her—a long, sensual kiss. When they broke apart, Lynn pressed the back of her head against the seat, closed her eyes and took in several calming breaths.

"Let's get out of here."

The only response she was capable of giving him was a weak nod. He started the engine and zoomed through the streets at breakneck speed as if he couldn't get her away from there fast enough. Lynn had no idea where

he was driving. Her mind was whirling. Marriage. Ryder was offering her marriage because he couldn't see
any way around it. Yet he claimed he loved her...loved
the kids.

The biggest problem that Lynn faced was her feelings for Ryder. She hadn't had time to analyze what was
happening between them. If he was looking to rescue
her, she didn't need that. Nor did she want to negate any
lingering guilt he was suffering over Gary's death.

Yet in her heart she loved Ryder...she always had.
However, her feelings for him were deeply rooted in
friendship from years past when she, Ryder and Gary
had spent so much time together. In the years since Ryder had been away, her love for him had gone dormant. But now that he was back, it was as if he'd never
left, although her love had been transformed from that
between a sister for a brother to that between a woman
and a man. Everything was magically different and had
been from the moment he'd first kissed her. Her whole
world had changed drastically.

"You don't seem to have much to say," he commented, his voice gruff. "Lynn, listen, I don't mean to
rush you. When we started out tonight, I had no intention of proposing, but it seemed the right thing to do."

"In the heat of the moment?"

"No!"

"It isn't necessary, you know."

"What? Marrying you?"

"Yes." She couldn't believe she was admitting
something like this. She'd held on to her virtue with
steel manacles with every other man she'd dated, but
one touch from Ryder and she'd never felt more alive.
It was as if her whole body had been hibernating for

three long years, and suddenly every cell had sprung to life.

"It's what I want."

Lynn couldn't understand why. His brief affairs had been legendary, but he didn't seem to want a short-term commitment from her. And from the dark scowl that covered his face, she realized he was offering her all or nothing.

"I'm not looking for an affair with you, Lynn."

That message had come through loud and clear the day at the waterworks park. "But, Ryder—"

"Do you or do you not want to get married?" The question was sharp with impatience.

Lynn squared her shoulders. "I'm not looking for anyone to rescue me."

His laugh was short and sarcastic. "You're telling me? Every time I so much as try, you bite my head off and calmly take control."

"And if you think you owe me something because of what happened to Gary—"

"Gary has nothing to do with this." Once more his words were sharp and abrupt.

Lynn gnawed on her bottom lip. Indecision boiled inside her. No clear direction presented itself.

"Are you going to marry me and put us both out of this misery?"

His voice was tender and warm, scattering Lynn's objections before she had a chance to assemble them. "I . . . think so." She would be a fool to turn him down and equally foolish to agree. She felt like laughing and crying at once. Good God, what was she doing?

Ryder stepped on the brake, reached for her and kissed her soundly, ravaging her mouth. "I'll take that as a yes, then."

Lynn's mind was spinning. "We need to talk, though, don't you think?"

"Fine. A week from Saturday, okay?"

"You want to wait that long to talk?"

He cast her an astonished glance. "No, get married."

"So soon?" she gasped.

Ryder frowned. "As far as I'm concerned, it's a week longer than I want to wait. I'm going out of my head wanting you this way." He turned off the familiar thoroughfare and headed toward her house, easing the car into the driveway, out of sight of the house and hidden from the neighbors.

The engine had barely had time to stop humming before Ryder reached for her, closing his arms convulsively around her shoulders. Lynn wordlessly lifted her face to him, reaching out to him, parting her lips, shamelessly inviting his kiss. It was hot and possessive.

"Invite me inside," he muttered, nibbling on the edges of her lips.

"The kids?"

"We'll send them to bed."

She nodded, eager for his touch.

As it happened, both Michelle and Jason were upstairs asleep. Lynn paid the baby-sitter and walked the teenager to the door. She stood on the porch until the neighbor girl was safely inside her own house. By the time Lynn returned to the kitchen, Ryder was brewing a pot of coffee.

"I don't want that," she told him, slipping her arms around his middle, feeling brazen. When she accepted his proposal, she'd experienced a release of sorts. She was taking a chance marrying Ryder, but then life was full of them, and living dangerously entailed a good deal of excitement.

"You don't want any coffee?"

"Nope." She skillfully dealt with the buttons of his shirt. Once it was opened, she rubbed her palms up his firm chest, reveling in the feel of his nakedness.

Ryder's hands were equally busy. Their bodies were on fire for each other as they explored, beseeched and promised all at the same time.

"Say it," Ryder growled hoarsely. "I need to hear you say it."

At the moment, she would have agreed to verbalize anything he wanted. "What?" she asked, bewildered. "I'll marry you? I already said I would. Next week, tomorrow. Tonight, if you want."

"Not that." He kissed her repeatedly, slipping his hands down over her buttocks, letting her feel his obvious desire.

She whimpered softly. "Ryder, what?"

"Tell me you love me. I need to hear the words... I need to know what you feel for me."

With her hands braced against the curve of his neck, she paused and slowly lifted her head. Her hungry gaze met his, and she was astonished at the uneasiness she saw there. He didn't know. He honest to God didn't know.

A savage tenderness tore through her. This was a man who had often been recognized for his determination and arrogance. A man bold and persistent, volatile and tenacious. Yet he'd made himself vulnerable to her, opened himself up, exposed his inner self in a way she had never dreamed possible.

She slipped her hands up his neck and laced her fingers through his hair. His eyes held her, watching her, loving her. Tears boiled beneath the surface of her eyes.

"Lynn?"

She cocked her head at an angle to his mouth and slowly, patiently kissed him, slipping her tongue inside his mouth. He groaned, securing her against him.

"I love you," she told him when she'd finished the kiss. "I love you," she repeated obligingly when she witnessed a flicker of doubt flash into his gaze. "For now ... for always."

"Dear God, Lynn," he cried, and buried his face in her neck, crushing her in his embrace. "I need you so much."

Lynn doubted that she'd ever heard any words more beautiful in her life.

Lynn hardly slept that night and woke early the next morning, feeling rummy and out of sorts. A woman in love, a woman who had agreed to marry a man she'd loved and admired, shouldn't be feeling like this.

When the first light of dawn peeled across a cranky sky, Lynn climbed out of bed and stumbled into the kitchen to make a pot of coffee.

By all rights, she should be the happiest woman alive. Between kisses and the building enthusiasm for this marriage, she'd agreed to a wedding date less than ten days away, although she couldn't understand the rush. But Ryder had been insistent and she couldn't find it in her heart to delay the ceremony any longer than he wanted. Yet she couldn't understand why he felt the need to bulldoze her into marriage.

Ryder had left her in the early morning hours when she'd been high on his love. She'd watched him leave and had reluctantly gone to bed. It was then that this melancholy mood had settled over her.

Their time together had been splurged on kisses and promises. They'd only brushed over the truly important issues. There were so many things that needed to be settled. Slender, Too, was a big concern to Lynn. She didn't want to give up her business and she feared Ryder might insist upon certain changes. If he did, there could be problems. The children worried her, too. They loved Ryder, but he'd always played the role of an indulgent uncle with them. A father...stepfather was something entirely different, and she would personally feel more comfortable having him ease into that role instead of being thrust upon Michelle and Jason unexpectedly this way.

"Mom." Jason stood just inside the kitchen, looking surprised to see her. "What are you doing up so early?"

"Thinking," she answered with a smile. She held out her arms for a hug. He gave her one, although reluctantly. It was on her mind to tell him Rambo hugged his mother, but she let the thought slide.

As for her answer to his question, he seemed to find the fact that she'd gotten up early to "think" acceptable. He dragged a chair across the kitchen floor, stood on it and opened the cupboard above the refrigerator, bringing down a cereal box. He then proceeded to pour himself a huge bowl.

"I thought we were out of Cap'n Crunch cereal?"

"That's what I wanted Michelle to think," he whispered. "A girl can't appreciate the finer qualities this cereal has to offer a man."

"So you've been holding out on her?"

He hesitated. "If that's the way you want to think of it."

At another time, Lynn would have scolded her son for his selfishness. Instead she decided to forego the lecture, determined to buy two boxes of the kids' favorite cereal the next time she went grocery shopping. That would settle that problem.

"So how'd the date go with Ryder?" Jason asked, carrying the impossibly full bowl over to the table and plopping himself down beside her.

"It . . . was nice."

"Nice?" Jason repeated, crunching his cereal at breakneck speed.

"Jason, please, don't talk with your mouth full."

"Sorry." He wiped the sleeve of his camouflage pajamas across his mouth. "So you had a good time?"

"We had a very nice time."

"You like Ryder real well, don't you?" He paused and studied her, his dark brown eyes wide and curious.

"Yes . . ."

"Good," he said and nodded once, profoundly.

"Why is that good?"

His gaze darted across the room, skirting her probing one. "Because."

That didn't explain a whole lot. She was about to comment when Michelle appeared, looking sleepy and cross. "Good morning, sweetheart," Lynn greeted.

Michelle grunted in reply, walked past her mother and brother, crisscrossed her legs, plopped herself down in front of the sink and opened the cupboard. Lynn leaned backward in her chair to watch what her daughter was doing and nearly laughed out loud when Michelle extracted a box of Cap'n Crunch cereal from behind the pipes.

Jason's mouth dropped open. "She's been holding out on me," he fumed, glaring at his mother. "Aren't you going to say something?"

Lynn glanced from one child to the other and slowly shook her head. "No way—I'm staying out of this one."

Jason slouched forward, and muttered something under his breath about what kind of mother had God assigned him, anyway!

By midmorning, Lynn had come to a decision. She would agree to marry Ryder, but to do so within ten days was impossible. She would insist they set the date several weeks in the future, possibly in three or four months. Marriage was what they both wanted, but she couldn't understand Ryder's need to rush into a relationship this important. They had the rest of their lives to spend together, and lots of questions that needed to be answered before sealing their vows.

A niggling fear kept cropping up in the back of Lynn's mind. From the first day he'd returned, Ryder had resisted discussing Gary. Anytime Gary's name was mentioned, Ryder found a way to change the subject.

Although he'd assured her otherwise, Lynn couldn't dismiss the fear that Ryder was marrying her and taking on the responsibility of raising Michelle and Jason out of some kind of warped idea of duty and her dead husband. She honestly didn't believe that was the case, but the thought troubled her and she wanted the issue cleared.

At noon, she took the time to phone Ryder. She frowned when the honey-voiced receptionist answered. Whoever she was, the woman was efficient, and Lynn was connected with Ryder's office immediately.

"Lynn." Ryder sounded pleased to hear from her.

"Hi," she managed to swallow the question about the age of the receptionist. She was behaving like a jealous fool. Simply because the woman's voice sounded like black velvet didn't mean she looked like a beauty queen. "Would it be possible for you to stop over at the house tonight?"

"Of course. Any reason?"

"I . . . I think we should talk, don't you?"

He chuckled softly. "We don't seem to be able to do much of that, do we?"

Lynn blushed and whispered. "No, but I think we should try."

"I'll be out of here at about three. Do you want me to pick up Michelle and Jason for you?"

The way things were looking at the salon, that might be a good idea. "If you don't mind."

"I don't," he assured her.

"I'll be done here around six."

"The kids and I'll be waiting for you," he paused. "Everything's all right, isn't it?"

Lynn couldn't see stirring up trouble over the phone. "Of course."

"We're going to have a good life, Lynn. A damn good life."

Lynn didn't doubt Ryder, but she had her fears and she wanted them laid to rest. A lengthy engagement wouldn't hurt either of them.

By the time she arrived at the house, Ryder's car was parked out front. She pulled into the driveway and had no sooner climbed out of the driver's side when both kids and Ryder appeared.

"Why didn't you tell us?" Michelle cried, bouncing up and down with excitement.

"Tell you what, honey?" Ryder would know better than to say anything to the kids about their wedding plans. The task was for her and her alone. Nonetheless, she frowned, wondering.

She slapped her hands against her thighs. "About you and Ryder getting married next week. Mom, this is just wonderful."

Lynn's narrowed gaze flew to Ryder.

"I told you this would happen," Jason told his sister with a look of untainted righteousness. "Even when you wouldn't sign the pact in blood, it worked. They're getting married just the way we want them to."

Fifteen

"Ryder," Lynn whispered angrily. "What have you done?"

"We called and talked to the pastor," Michelle informed her mother with a cheerful grin. "He said next Saturday is fine with him, and then Ryder called the florist. You're really going to love all the roses and stuff."

Jason examined a caterpillar he was holding in the palm of his hand. "Grandma sounded surprised, though, don't you think, Michelle?"

"You've talked to your grandparents?"

"I know they're supposed to be on vacation, but I figured you'd want them to know. They're packing up the motor home and driving back to Seattle right away."

"Oh, dear God." Lynn slumped against the side of her car.

"You're happy, aren't you, Mom?"

"I..."

"I think we may be moving too fast for your mother, but I didn't want to give her a chance to change her mind." Ryder's eyes reached out and gently caressed Lynn.

"She's not going to back out," Michelle quickly assured him. "We won't let her."

"I...I think Ryder and I've got several issues we need to settle first, though," she said through clenched teeth.

"Aren't you going to give her the ring?" Jason asked, tugging at Ryder's sleeve. Her son turned toward Lynn. "It's been in his family for seventy years. This is the engagement ring his grandfather gave his grandmother and his father his mother. I think this may mean you're going to have babies, right?"

Lynn opened her mouth, but she didn't know how to answer Jason. The subject of children was one in a long list she had yet to discuss with Ryder.

"I wouldn't mind a brother," Jason informed her, "but I don't know what I'd do with another sister. I wouldn't suppose there's any way you could order me a baby boy?"

"Jason," Michelle demanded, jerking him away. "Can't you see Mom and Ryder need time alone? He wants to give her the ring."

"I'm going to watch. It isn't every day a kid gets to see this kind of mushy stuff." The eight-year-old yanked his elbow from his sister's grasp and refused to budge. "Ryder's marrying us, too—we should get to see this if we want."

"I'd like more children." Ryder's dark eyes continued to hold Lynn's, his gaze filled with tenderness.

The word *more* was her undoing. Ryder honestly loved Michelle and Jason, as though he had actually fathered them. In the future she need never doubt that his actions weren't prompted by genuine concern for their welfare.

"Are you going to tell her about us moving into another house?" Michelle questioned.

"Another house?" Infuriated, Lynn swerved toward her daughter. She felt as if every aspect of her life had been taken over. "Do you have any *other* surprises for me?"

"I think I'd better do the talking now," Ryder said with a halting smile. His hand at the small of Lynn's back directed her toward the front door, although Lynn tried to free herself. Rushing her into an early wedding was one thing, but making these kind of arrangements was going too far. Worlds too far. Her mind was whirling with outrage.

"Ryder, just what the hell is going on?" She whirled around the instant she was inside the door. "You've contacted my parents in Minnesota, you've talked to the pastor and ordered flowers—"

"You object?"

"You're damn right I do." She was fighting like mad to quell her anger. The last thing she wanted was for her children to witness what she planned to him. Fury and words were nearly foaming at her mouth. But Michelle and Jason worshiped the man and if she was going to have a heated argument with him, she would rather they were out of hearing distance. Besides, knowing her children, they would probably side with Ryder!

"I was only trying to help."

"You weren't," she nearly shouted. "You're forcing me into this wedding and I don't like it. Not one damn bit."

Jason scooted a chair from the kitchen, twisted it around and straddled it as if it were a wild bronco. He propped his chin in his hands, his gaze shifting from Ryder to his mother and then back again.

"Jason, I need to talk to Ryder . . . alone."

"Sure." But he didn't budge.

"I think your mother wants you to leave, son," Ryder explained a minute later.

"Oh." Jason hopped off the chair, looking mildly chagrined. "Michelle told me you were going to fight, but she said that's something moms and dads do all the time and there wasn't any need to worry."

"There's nothing to be concerned about."

Ryder answered the youngster when Lynn didn't. As far as she was concerned, there was *plenty* to be worried about. She waited until Jason had vacated the entryway.

"The whole thing's off," she announced, her hands slicing the air like an umpire making a call, his decision final.

It took a minute for Ryder to react. "All right, if that's what you want."

It wasn't entirely, but Lynn wasn't going to be railroaded into marriage.

She opened her mouth to tell him exactly how furious she was, but he turned his back to her and calmly stated, "Then we'll just have to live in sin."

"What?" she exploded.

"With the way things are between us now, you don't honestly expect us to stay out of the bedroom? We can try—we've done it so far, but my restraint is at its limit. You're probably stronger than me."

"I..." She looked over her shoulder to make sure Jason wasn't spying on them. "That's the least of my concerns. We're talking about blending our lives together. There are going to be problems."

"Like what?" He turned back to face her, hands in his pockets, the picture of nonchalance.

"Like... the kids. They love you now because you take them places, buy them things. You're like Santa Claus and the Easter Bunny all rolled into one wonderful person. But how are they going to feel when you start disciplining them?''

''That's something we're going to have to work out, isn't it?''

''In time, right.''

''You mean you won't marry me if the kids balk when I send them to bed and they don't want to go?''

Lynn folded her arms tightly around her stomach. ''I didn't suggest that . . . quit twisting everything I say to suit your own purpose.''

''I'm only answering your questions. I don't understand the problem with the kids. They know I love them, they trust me to be fair. What's going to change if we get married?''

''What about children? Jason started asking me about a baby brother and I didn't know how to answer him.''

''Do you want more children?''

''I think so . . . if you do.''

''I do. That settles that. Is there anything else?''

''What about Slender, Too? I've put a lot of time and effort into building it up and I don't want to walk away from it now.''

''You're asking me if I'm going to object if you keep working? Not in the least. That's your business and you have a right to be proud of what you've accomplished. I'm not going to take that away from you.''

The hot wind that had buoyed the sails of her outrage started to slacken. What had once threatened to be a hurricane force diminished to a gentle breeze.

''But I don't want you to overdo it,'' Ryder warned. ''When we decide it's time for you to get pregnant, I'd like you to consider taking time off to properly take care of yourself and the baby, but I'll leave that up to you.''

Lynn blinked and nodded. "Naturally I'd want to do that."

"I love you, Lynn. I want you for my wife."

She stared at him mesmerized as he straightened and walked toward her. He was impossible to resist when he was looking at her with his eyes filled with such love. The only thing Lynn had to quell at the moment was the impulse to fall into his arms.

"You're going to marry me, aren't you?" he asked on a husky murmur. "It's what we both want, but yet you keep fighting it. Why?"

"I'm afraid," she admitted.

"I frighten you that much?"

"Not you," she countered.

"What then?"

Now that she had the opportunity to voice her objections, she found them garbled and twisted in her mind. If she were to mention Gary's name, he would tell her how silly she was being in the same way that he'd assured her about everything else.

"Gary..."

Ryder frowned. "What about him?"

"You loved him?"

"You know I did."

As always when she mentioned Gary's name, Ryder tensed, but she had to know. "You're not marrying me out of a sense of duty, are you?"

His face twisted into a glower as if he resented her insinuating as much. "No," he answered abruptly. "I already told you I've dealt with the guilt of what happened. Loving you is completely separate from Gary's death."

"I...I had to be sure."

He reached for her, hauling her into his arms, his mouth seeking hers. She met his lips eagerly, returning the passion until she was weak and clinging. Because he'd turned her mind around so completely, she was frustrated they couldn't be married any sooner.

"You're going to marry me." This time it was a statement, not a question.

Lynn lowered her gaze and nodded. God help her for being such a fool, but she loved this man. He was offering her a piece of heaven and it wasn't in her to refuse.

"Michelle." Jason cried and popped up from behind the living-room sofa. "It's working out just great."

Lynn slumped forward, securing her forehead against Ryder's chest. "He was listening the whole time."

"Hurry and come downstairs," Jason yelled. "We don't have anything to worry about . . . they're getting married just the way you said. We're going to be a real family in no time."

"Do you take this man to be your lawfully wedded husband?" Pastor Teed asked Lynn.

She stared up at Ryder, who was standing so confidently beside her, and felt her insides go soft, and her heart began to pound unnaturally hard. She was about to make a giant leap into a whole new life. She stood tall and proud, but on the inside she was a mass of quivering nerves.

"Lynn," the pastor prompted softly.

"I do," she returned, certain that she was doing the right thing.

Ryder smiled at her and although the man of God continued speaking, Lynn barely heard what he was saying. When Pastor Teed informed Ryder that he could kiss the bride, he did so gently, as if she were the most priceless piece of porcelain in the world and he feared breaking her. Silly tears gathered in the corners of her eyes. She had never expected to find such happiness and love a second time—she'd given up trying. Yet here she was standing before God and man, pledging her life to Ryder.

The reception was an intimate affair with only a handful of friends. Her parents were there, and Toni Morris, who was busy serving cake and coffee. Lynn's mother and father looked happy and proud. They knew Ryder from before and were pleased with her choice.

Michelle and Jason mingled with the guests, telling everyone who would listen how they'd known all along that their mother was going to marry Ryder.

All too soon the reception came to a close, and it was time for Lynn to change out of the pale silk dress she'd worn for the wedding ceremony and into one more suitable for traveling.

Toni Morris wiped a stray tear from her cheek and hugged Lynn after she'd changed outfits. It was unlike Toni to be demonstrative and Lynn hugged her friend back, squeezing her tightly.

"I'm happy for you, Lynn. Ryder loves you, don't ever doubt that."

Lynn nodded, grateful for all the moral support Toni had given her over the years, although she found her friend's words mildly disturbing. There wasn't any reason for her to doubt Ryder's love.

"You've got everything?" Toni asked.

"Yes. I've been through the list a dozen times."

"Your parents are keeping Michelle and Jason for the week."

Sixteen

As bold as she'd been earlier in their courtship, Lynn felt like a blushing bride when she met Ryder in front of the reception hall at the country club.

"Bye, Mom," Michelle cried, hugging her mother tightly around the waist. "You'll bring me something back from Hawaii, won't you?"

"Of course."

In front of an audience, Jason wasn't as keen about showing his affection. He offered his mother his hand to shake, and Lynn politely shook it, then hugged him anyway.

"I'll bring you back something, too," she assured him before he could ask.

"Do you think you could find me a shark's jaw?"

Lynn cringed and nodded, knowing Jason would be delighted with the grisly bone. "I'll see what I can do."

Her mother and father stepped forward and Lynn gave them each a warm embrace, grateful, as always, for their unfailing love and support.

No more than a minute later, Lynn and Ryder were in his car on the way to a hotel close to the airport. Their flight was scheduled to leave for Honolulu early the following morning. Ryder had arranged for them to spend their first night in the honeymoon suite.

He reached for her hand and raised it to his mouth, kissing her fingertips. ''You're a beautiful bride, Mrs. Matthews.''

''Thank you.'' Once more she felt soft color flush into her cheeks. She was trembling and grateful that Ryder was too preoccupied with the traffic to notice her nervousness. There had only been one lover in her life and fears crowded the edges of her mind that she wouldn't be the kind of woman Ryder needed in bed. She would have preferred it if their lovemaking had happened more...naturally. She felt timid and shy and awkward with this man she had just married. It was right for them to wait, Lynn realized that much, but doubts confronted her at every turn. Not if she'd done the right thing by marrying Ryder, but if she was woman enough to satisfy him.

While Ryder registered them at the hotel desk, Lynn looked toward the four-star restaurant where several couples were dining by candlelight and champagne music. Ryder joined her a moment later.

''Hungry?''

She nodded eagerly, looking for a way to delay their lovemaking. She was being silly, she knew that, but she couldn't seem to shake her nervousness.

''We can order dinner from room service,'' Ryder suggested.

''Would you mind if we ate at the restaurant... here?'' she asked quickly.

Ryder looked disappointed, but agreed.

Lynn ordered two glasses of wine with her meal and showed more interest in the chardonnay than the shrimp stuffed sole. She lingered over dessert, ignoring the fact that Ryder preferred not to order any and glanced at his watch two or three times while she leisurely nibbled away at hers.

"There's nothing to worry about, you know," he whispered, after the waiter refilled her coffee cup for the third time.

Her head shot upward, her eyes round. "What...do you mean?"

"You know what I'm talking about."

"Ryder...my stomach feels like a nest of red ants are building a whole new colony in there. My palms are sweaty and I feel like an inexperienced girl. I want to make love with you so much it frightens me and yet I'm terrified of doing so."

"Honey, come on. There's only one way to face something like this."

"Maybe we should wait until we get to Hawaii... that's the real start of our honeymoon."

"Lynn, you're being ridiculous." He paid the bill and with his hand under her elbow, directing her, he led her to the elevator.

The whole way up to the twentieth floor, Lynn's mind floundered, seeking excuses. Never in a thousand years would she have believed she could be this anxious over something she'd been wanting for weeks. For heaven's sake, she'd practically seduced Ryder that day in the water.

Her husband opened the room and pushed open the door. He lifted her into his arms and, disregarding her protests, carried her into the opulent suite. Gently he set her back on the thick carpeting. Their suitcases were waiting for them on the floor next to the bed, but her gaze refused to go as far as the king-size mattress.

"Oh, look, they show movies," she said cheerfully, as though watching HBO would be the highlight of this trip.

"We're going to take things nice and slow, Lynn. There won't be any time for movies."

She nodded, realizing how incredibly absurd she must have sounded.

Reaching for her, Ryder took her shoulders between his hands and drew her against him. "I love you."

"I love you, too." Lynn tried to smile, she honestly tried, but she failed utterly. Moistening her lips, she lifted her arms, bracing her hands against his chest. The heavy beat of his heart seemed to thunder against her palms and did little to reassure her.

"There's magic between us," he told her in a warm whisper. "I recognized it the first time we kissed."

Lynn had, too. She stared into his tanned, lean face, loving him all the more for his patience. He smiled at her so gently, so tenderly, the way a child does when petting a newborn kitten. Lynn felt the worst of the tension ease out of her stiff body.

He kissed her, lightly, making no demands on her, then pulled away, studying her. "That wasn't so terrible, was it?"

She shut her eyes. "I'm making a fool of myself."

"No, you're not," he countered and kissed her again, more deeply this time, although he continued to hold her as though she were delicate and could easily break.

The taste of his mouth over hers was an awakening for Lynn, and as a brilliantly colored marigold does to the morning sun, Lynn opened to Ryder, flowering, seeking his warmth and love. There was nothing to be afraid of with this man. Nothing. The memory of his touch, the sound and taste of his lovemaking filled her mind. Thread by thread, the thoughts unwove her hesitation.

Ryder's gaze moved over her face. "Feeling better now?"

Lynn nodded. "Isn't it a little warm in here?" Before he could answer, she reached up and started unfastening the buttons of his starched white shirt.

"Now that you mention it, yes." Eagerly he shucked his suit coat and let it fall heedlessly to the floor. Lynn smiled to herself, knowing how unlike Ryder it was to be messy or disorganized.

He reached for the zipper at the back of her dress, easing it down, slowly, cautiously as though he expected her to bolt and run from him at any time. His shirt front was open and Lynn lifted her palms to his bare chest. His skin was hot to the touch and she longed to feel the kinky soft hairs matted there, against her face.

Ryder lifted his hands to her neck, easing the material of her dress over her shoulders and down her torso, past her hips. It disrupted her momentarily to step out of it and do away with her slip, bra and her other underthings, but they were disposed of soon enough.

She lifted her hands back to his chest. The need to taste him dominated her thoughts and she ran the tip of her tongue in a meandering path across his chest, savoring the hot, salty flavor of him.

Ryder shuddered and closed his arms around her waist, tugging her against his naked torso. She wrapped her arms around his neck, clinging to him, busying her fingers in the thick, dark hair at his nape. As she brushed her body against his, she could feel the gentle rasp of his body hair against her naked breasts.

"Oh, Ryder," she whispered in rapturous awe.

Somehow he moved them onto the bed, laying above her, lowering himself just enough to brush his chest over the tantalizing tips of her nipples. "Does that feel good, love?"

"Oh, yes . . . very good."

He stroked her breasts in a feather-light touch, lingering over each nipple until they quivered and throbbed. He moved his hand lower, and Lynn had to bite into her bottom lip to keep from moaning at the delicious, carnal stroke of his fingertips. She relaxed when he flattened his palm against her stomach. Then gradually, without her hardly noticing, he lowered his hand toward the area that was quickly becoming the pulsating center of her being. Unconsciously Lynn opened herself to him, parting her thighs.

Slowly, willfully, he moved his fingers to take intimate possession of her, exploring the innermost part of her body. As he slipped inside her, a soft, mewling sound rose from deep within her throat.

"How does that feel?" he asked in a hoarse whisper.

"Oh, Ryder. Good . . . so good."

He lowered his mouth to her breast and suckled at one pebbled nipple. The hot sensation that shot through her was incredible, indescribable. It was as though the two parts of her body where he was centering his attention were somehow irrevocably linked. Electricity arced between her nipples and her womanhood and she whimpered softly as waves of fiery pleasure washed over her body.

Ryder's mouth found hers in a kiss that was hard, hot and coaxing. He kissed her with a fierceness that robbed her of her breath and caused the blood to pound through her veins. She willingly parted her lips, gladly admitting the conquering hero of his tongue as it swept inside her mouth. She arched her back, and her tingling breasts encountered the hard, hairy wall of his chest once more.

"Ryder," she moaned, "I want you so much."

"Not yet, love."

Desire for him rocked through her until she was certain if he didn't take her soon, her bones would melt, longing for him the way she did. Her heart was pounding harder than it had at any other time in her life. Each staccato beat's echo was magnified a hundredfold in her ears.

His lips continued to torture her nipples exquisitely until the yearning was so potent she thought she would die from wanting him. It saturated every cell of her being and she lifted his head, and raised her mouth to his, longing to show him with her kiss how eager she was to be his wife. All her nervous reserve was gone, evaporating under his tender ministrations.

"Oh . . . please," she begged.

Her words broke his restraint and with a cry of triumph, he covered her with his body. She felt his desire, urgent and incredibly hard against her. With one swift motion, he spread her thighs and lowered himself inside her to the hilt with a single push.

Lynn moaned as the waves of pleasure swayed over her.

He stopped, breathlessly. "I hurt you."

"No . . . no." She lifted her arms, folded them around his neck and spread moist kisses over his mouth and face. "I love you . . . love you."

Ryder started to move in a swift unbroken rhythm, but soon stopped, his breath making hissing sounds through his clenched teeth.

Lynn's eyes flew open and she discovered Ryder with his head tossed back, eyes squeezed tight, battling for control of his body. Unable to resist, Lynn rotated her hips once.

"No... no," he pleaded. "Don't move."

She placed her hands on his pronounced hipbones and slowly, seductively raised her derriere in a flurry of movements that served to draw him deeper inside her.

Ryder released a tremendous groan.

Lynn tangled her fingers in his hair and he dropped forward enough for her to plant a wild kiss on his lips. Her tongue darted inside his mouth and she gloried in the way his body trembled above hers.

She realized there was no holding him back any longer, and smiled contentedly at his cry of triumph as he thrust forward. He crushed her body to his, his breath scalding and broken as he quickly reached his apex.

"Lynn... oh, Lynn." He collapsed on top of her, planting swift kisses on her eyes, mouth and neck.

She was replete, utterly enraptured by sensation.

Then they slept in each other's arms, and when she awoke the room was filled with dark shadows of night. She felt wonderful and, raising herself up on her elbow, she watched her husband's face, relaxed now in sleep. He looked almost boyish and the surge of love that rocked through her brought a rush of tears to her eyes.

Slipping out of the sheet, she moved into the bathroom and ran water for a bath, luxuriating in the hot liquid.

"Lynn?" A thread of panic filled his voice.

"I'm in here." She climbed out of the tub and reached for a towel, holding it against her breasts.

Ryder stumbled into the room, looking mussed and sleepy, but he paused and relaxed when he saw her. "You're beautiful, Mrs. Matthews," he said, leaning against the door.

"I didn't mean to wake you."

"I'm glad you did."

"You are?"

He took a step toward her and gently pulled away the towel she was holding against her water-slickened body. "You're even more beautiful now."

Lynn lowered her head.

"You doubt me?"

"No," she told him softly. "Telling me that only assures me how much you really *do* love me." When she glanced at him, she read the confusion in his eyes. "I'm over thirty, Ryder, and I've borne two children... they've left their marks on my body. I'm not going to win any beauty pageants."

Instead of arguing, Ryder reached for her, folding her in his embrace. He led her back into the bedroom. "There isn't a woman on this earth more beautiful to me than you." His voice shook with sincerity.

He sat on the edge of the mattress and pulled her down into his lap. He lifted his hands to her hair and tugged it loose from the carefully braided French roll the hairdresser had spent so many hours creating for her wedding. The length fell down the middle of her back. Ryder parted it over her shoulder and the dark length hung loosely, nearly covering the tips of her breasts.

He paused and seemed to stop breathing as he lifted it away from her head with widespread fingers, letting the softness flow through his hands like spilled coffee. "I've dreamed of you kissing me with your hair falling over my face."

With her hands at his shoulders, she gently pressed him back against the mattress, securing him there. He watched her with curious eyes as she positioned herself above him, her legs braced on both sides of his hips.

Slowly, very slowly, she leaned forward, letting her hair fall over him. But Ryder surprised her even more by raising his head and clamping his arm around her waist. His open mouth landed with damp impact on her breast and he suckled greedily. He slid his hands downward and stroked her bare bottom as he brought his lips from one breast to the other until she whimpered with the explosive desire that pitched through her.

Lynn curled her fingers around Ryder's ears as he branded her breasts with hot, ardent kisses, sucking greedily at their tips. A desire so potent that it seemed beyond understanding saturated her and, as if mesmerized, she lowered her mouth toward him. As their lips met, she inhaled the exciting scent that was his alone. She wanted to fulfill his fantasy and shook her head several times until her dark curls fell over his face. By twisting her head one way and then another, she was able to fan her hair across his face and chest.

"Oh, Lynn," he breathed, planting his hands on her sides and arching his hips. The most intimate parts of their bodies made contact and they both went instantly still.

After a moment, Lynn slowly brought up her head, taking in deep breaths to control her desire, but she nearly drowned in languid sensation when Ryder slipped his finger inside her once more. He worked his special brand of magic, discovering all her secrets, unlocking the doors of inhibition. Unable to stop herself, she moved against him, rotating her hips back and forth, her eyes closed.

"Ryder." She repeated his name again and again, as he stroked her into a private universe where the sun and the moon were hers alone. Joy, love and exquisite pleasure pulsed through her as she cried out his name and sagged on top of him, savoring the spasms of release that gripped her.

Her bare thighs hugged his waist. Lynn was amazed at how expertly he switched their positions so that he was poised above her. Without waiting, he glided smoothly into her body. Holding himself still, he lowered his mouth to hers, his eyes ablaze, his lips hot and devouring. A sudden thrust buried him deeper yet and Lynn tossed her head to one side, reveling in the wild sensations his actions commanded.

He began to move then, slowly, taking his time, savoring each individual stroke until Lynn lay gasping and trembling, climbing ever higher to the spiraling, inexplicable madness that took control of her body.

She draped her arms around his neck and strained upward, reveling in the feel of the tight muscles of his chest. Ryder locked his arms around her back. She ran her fingers through his hair and pulled his mouth down to hers, tugging at his tongue in a kiss that was both carnal and wild.

She felt his climax and whimpered with joy. Nothing had ever been this good. Nothing had ever given her the incredible feeling Ryder did.

He released her by degrees, lowering her onto the mattress a little at a time while he pressed kisses onto her shoulder. Her teeth marked his shoulder in playful bites. He shifted his weight so he was lying beside her. He leaned forward just enough to kiss her, his features softened by his contentment.

Lynn yawned and tried to cover her mouth, but Ryder wouldn't let her.

"So I bore you."

She smiled lazily. "If that's the case, you have permission to pester me anytime you want."

"I plan on doing exactly that," he whispered before closing his eyes and falling into a deep, undisturbed slumber.

Ryder scooted his chair away from his desk. He should be going over a brief, but his mind refused to focus on the case he was studying. Instead, his thoughts drifted to his wife. They'd been married for several weeks now and it was as if they'd always been together. Every time he thought about Lynn his throat filled with such strong emotion that he could hardly breathe. He couldn't get enough of her and her special brand of lovemaking. Every time he felt her body, all soft and athletic beside him, it affected him. He had to have her. Sometimes once a night wasn't enough. Lynn seemed as eager as he was for this side of their marriage and that pleased him immeasurably. He would reach for her and she would come into his arms with an enthusiasm that caused his blood to boil.

Loving and craving Lynn the way he did frightened him. He'd never expected to experience this deep a commitment in his life. The need he felt just to know she was close clawed at him like vicious tentacles and the thought of losing her was enough to drive him over the edge of sanity.

He glanced at his watch, troubled by his thoughts. Lynn would be home by now. The hell with the brief, he would read it tonight. With that, he shoved the papers inside his briefcase and headed out of the office.

Lynn's car was parked in the driveway when he pulled up in front of the house and he exhaled sharply.

"You're home early," she greeted, when he stepped into the kitchen. She wore an apron around her waist and was slicing thin strips of beef for their dinner.

"Where are Michelle and Jason?" he asked, and slipped his arms around her waist, nuzzling her neck.

"Michelle's helping Janice baby-sit and will be home at five-thirty, and Jason's at soccer practice."

"Good." He unknotted the apron strings and let it drop to the kitchen floor.

"Ryder?"

Next, he fiddled with the buttons on her blouse, peeling it open with an excitement that caused his hands to shake. He began to massage her breasts in a leisurely circular motion until her nipples beaded, welcoming his attention.

Ryder had only meant to touch her, but the minute his hands experienced the silky softness of her skin he knew there was no stopping him. A melting sort of ecstasy grew within him that would be satisfied only by making love to Lynn.

"Now?" she breathed the question.

He answered her with an ardent kiss, cupping her buttocks and raising her off the floor just enough to fit her against his manhood and reveal without words his desire.

"Dinner's going to be late," she whispered.

"We'll order pizza," he answered, leading her toward the stairs.

Lynn giggled. "Ryder, we're too old for this! We can't keep this up and live beyond forty."

"Talk for yourself, woman."

* * *

"Married life certainly seems to suit you," Toni commented over lunch a few days later.

The lunch was Toni's treat. But Lynn wasn't fooled; her friend wanted to gloat. When Lynn had announced to Toni that she was marrying Ryder, Toni had asked what took her so long to figure out why Ryder had come back to Seattle.

"I'm so much in love I can hardly stand it," Lynn admitted almost shyly. "It's funny really...I'd given up dating. As far as I could see the world was filled with . . . I don't know."

"I think the term you used earlier this summer was warthogs."

Lynn smiled. "That about says it. Ryder came into my life when I least expected to fall in love again."

"I'd like to say I told you so, but Joe wouldn't let me say one word to you about Ryder loving you."

Lynn would have doubted her friend, anyway.

"Everything's working out with the kids?"

"It's too good to be true. They turn to him just as if he were their father. From day one they've both been on their best behavior."

"You don't expect that to last, do you?"

"No. Ryder knows that, too."

"Now what's this I hear about you buying a new house?"

Lynn focused her attention on the chef salad and slowly exhaled, hoping her friend didn't notice her hesitation. "Ryder wants to move."

"Is that so difficult to understand?"

It wasn't, but Lynn still had trouble letting go of the house. She'd lived in that colonial since shortly after she and Gary were married. Both children had been born while they lived there. The house was filled with happy memories of a life she treasured and revered. It was convenient to the salon and shopping. The school was only a few blocks away and the neighbors were good friends. At Ryder's insistence, they'd looked at several new homes, but Lynn couldn't find one that suited her.

"Is it?" Toni pressed.

"I can't seem to find anything I like."

"And Ryder?"

"He's found several he thinks we'll fit into nicely. We're leaning toward a five-bedroom place a couple of miles from where we live now."

"Five bedrooms?" Toni gasped, mocking Lynn with her eyes.

"Ryder wants one for a den."

"And later one for the baby?"

Lynn blushed. "There isn't going to be any baby for a year or more, so get that snide look off your face."

"But not from lack of trying, if what I see in your face is true. Good grief Lynn, it isn't any wonder Ryder's got circles under his eyes and you walk around wearing that silly grin."

"Toni, stop it, you're embarrassing me." But she *was* wearing a smile these days, a contented one, and nothing seemed to dampen her good spirits.

"How's the salon doing?"

Lynn shrugged. "Good. I've got a membership campaign in the works. I'm training a couple of new girls who seem to be working out nicely—no pun intended. Things couldn't be better."

"And Ryder doesn't object to you spending so much time at the salon?"

Lynn shrugged. There wasn't any reason for him to complain. She was home every night, usually before he was. He did offer a suggestion or two, which she'd taken into consideration. He liked to know what was going on in her business and she enjoyed sharing that part of her life with him.

"I hope you're not going to kill yourself over this membership campaign," Toni said with a sigh. "I know you and it's difficult for you to delegate responsibility. You can't do everything yourself, so don't make the mistake of trying."

The two chatted for several minutes more, then parted. Lynn went back to the salon, checked in with Sharon, then took the rest of the afternoon off, stopping at a couple of stores on the way home to do some shopping.

On impulse, she bought a negligee, wondering how long she would be able to keep it on once she modeled it for Ryder.

The house was quiet when she unlocked the door. Once inside the entryway, she turned, feeling that something wasn't right, but couldn't put her finger on it. She looked around, but didn't notice anything different. Ryder was still at the office and both kids were in school. She set down the grocery bags and placed the milk inside the refrigerator.

"Hi, Mom." Jason shouted as he came through the front door. The screen door slammed in his wake. "What's for snack?"

"Milk and—"

"Are we having pizza for dinner again tonight?"

Lynn tried to hide a smile. "Why?"

"Joey wants to come over for dinner if we are. He said he didn't know anyone in the whole world who had pizza four nights in a row."

"Actually I thought I'd serve spaghetti and meat-balls tonight. Is that all right?"

"Sure," he shrugged and reached for an apple. "I'm going outside, okay?"

"What about your homework?"

"I don't have any and if I did, I'd do it after dinner."

Lynn walked him to the front door and again was assailed with the fact that something was out of place. She turned and strolled through the living room, paused, and turned around.

Her gaze fell on the television and she gasped. Gary's picture, which had rested there for over three years was gone. She whirled around and looked at the fireplace. *All* the pictures of him were missing from there, too. Only the ones of her and Michelle and Jason remained.

There was only one person who would have removed them, and that was Ryder.

Lynn knew it was time for a talk.

Seventeen

"Hi, Mom," Michelle greeted when Lynn walked in the house the following week. Her daughter's gaze was glued to the television where a popular rock group was crooning out the unintelligible words to a top-ten hit.

Lynn ripped the sweatband from her forehead and hurried toward the kitchen, tossing her purse on the counter and rubbing the pain in the small of her back. "Where're Ryder and Jason?"

"Soccer practice."

Lynn heaved a sigh of relief—she should have remembered that. This was the third night in a row that she was late getting out of the salon and she'd been worried about confronting Ryder. He hadn't said anything about the extra hours she was putting in, but she knew it bothered him.

"What's for dinner?" Michelle yelled. "I'm starved."

Lynn rubbed her hand over her face and sighed. "I don't know yet."

"Mom...is it going to be another one of those nights?"

Lynn paused. "What do you mean by that?"

"The only time we have a decent meal anymore is when Ryder orders out."

Lynn wanted to argue, but she hadn't a leg to stand on, as the old saying went. Things had been hectic at Slender, Too, since the first of the month. Lynn had started a membership campaign with local newspaper and radio advertisement. The response had been greater than she'd dared to hope, but consequently she was left to deal with a ton of paperwork plus individual exercise programs to calculate for her newest customers. To complicate matters, Lynn had come up with the brilliant idea of hanging a star from the salon ceiling for every inch lost in the month of September. It sounded like such a good suggestion at the time. But her fingers ached from working with scissors and the salon was quickly beginning to resemble another planet.

"How does bacon, eggs and pancakes sound?" Lynn asked her daughter, forcing some enthusiasm into her voice.

"Like something you should serve for breakfast."

"Sometimes a breakfast meal can be fun at dinnertime." Rooting through the refrigerator didn't offer her any other suggestions. The shelves were bare. What leftovers there were had long been eaten.

"How about tacos?"

Jason would love that, and Lynn sighed her regret. "I don't have any hamburger thawed out."

"Use the microwave...what have you got in the freezer, anyway?"

"Bacon and that's it." Lynn had been so busy over the weekend that she hadn't had time to buy groceries. It was already Wednesday and she still hadn't gotten to the market.

"You mean to tell me all we've got is bacon?"

"I'm sorry," she snapped, "I'll get to the store tomorrow."

"That's what you said last night."

The front door banged open and Jason stormed inside like a Texas whirlwind. "I scored two goals and made an assist and Mr. Lawson said I did the best ever."

Lynn hugged her son and brushed the sweat-heavy hair from his flushed brow. "That's great."

"Ryder's going to be the assistant coach now."

Lynn's gaze found her husband's. "I didn't know you played soccer."

"He doesn't," Jason answered automatically, dismissing that detail as minor. "I have to teach him."

"But..." Lynn was about to question Ryder about the unexpectedness of his offer, when Jason jerked open the refrigerator and groaned.

"You haven't got any pop yet?"

"I... didn't get a chance to get to the store."

Jason wailed in protest. "Mom, you promised. I'm dying of thirst...you don't honestly expect me to drink *water*, do you?"

"I didn't promise. I told you I'd *try* to get to the store," she barked, feeling pressured and angry. "Why do I have to be the one to do everything around here? I work, too, you know. If I lazed around some luxurious office all day reading court papers then I'd probably have more time for other things, too." Lynn couldn't believe what she was saying, how unfair she was being, but once she got started, she couldn't seem to stop. Ryder was the one having fun with her children while she was stuck in her office cutting out stupid gold stars. Tears filled her eyes and when she wiped them aside, she found Michelle, Jason and Ryder all staring at her in stunned silence.

Both children stood frozen, their eyes wide with shock and horror. Ryder's gaze was spitting and angry, but outwardly, at least, he remained calm.

"I think your mother and I need some time alone," he told Michelle and Jason, his hands on their shoulders. Gently he guided them toward the stairs. There was a quick exchange of whispers before Ryder returned to the kitchen.

"That's it, Lynn," he told her when he returned.

She slammed a package of microwave-thawed bacon on the counter. "All right, I shouldn't have said that. I apologize." Her hands were furiously at work trying to peel the thick slices of meat apart and place them in the frying pan.

"That's not good enough." He took a step closer.

"Don't accept my apology, then." She refused to look at him, fearing she would burst into tears if she did. The ache in the small of her back intensified.

"It's been weeks since we returned from Hawaii. At first everything was wonderful, but it's been a nightmare ever since."

"How can you say that?" she cried. She'd been trying so hard to be a good wife to him. Not once had she turned him down when he wanted to make love . . . and heaven knew that was every night. She kept the house spotless, managed the laundry and everything else that kept the household running smoothly. Okay, she hadn't gotten groceries in a few days, but that was only a minor thing.

"For the past two weeks, you fly in here after six, throw something together for dinner and then collapse."

"I work hard." She felt like weeping, tears churned just below the surface and the knot forming in her throat was large enough to choke her. No one seemed to appreciate all she did—they simply took it for granted that she could keep up with everything. Well, she couldn't.

"We all work hard—Michelle and Jason, too, in their own way. I just don't like what you're doing to yourself and everyone close to you."

Ryder wasn't the only one with complaints. She had a few of her own. Because she'd been so busy at work, she hadn't even mentioned anything about Gary's pictures being missing. Nor had she said anything about how she felt Ryder was trying to buy Michelle's and Jason's love. He couldn't seem to do enough for them. This latest thing—agreeing to help coach Jason's soccer team when he knew next to nothing about the sport was a perfect example.

"You're exhausted," he complained. "Look at you. You can hardly stand, you're so tired. You keep driving yourself and pretty soon you're going to crack. I can't allow that, Lynn. You're too important to us."

"If you didn't keep me up half the night with your lusty demands, then I might get a decent night's sleep."

Ryder's face drained of color. Lynn had never seen a man look more furious. His eyes were as cold as glaciers and when they narrowed on her, she realized she'd stepped over the line of his patience.

"Come here, Lynn," he demanded in a voice that would have shattered diamonds.

"No."

He took the bacon out of her hand so fast that Lynn whirled around and gasped. The meat fell to the floor with a slapping sound that seemed to echo around the kitchen.

"Now look what you've done," she cried, backing away from him.

He cornered her against the counter, pinning her there with the full length of his body. Lynn glared at him, her chin raised, her eyes spitting with defiance. Tears continued to sting her eyes, but she would die before she let them fall.

"So it's my 'lusty demands' that are responsible for keeping you up all night?"

"Yes," she shouted.

"Then it's all my fault that you're so cranky and unreasonable."

She nodded, knowing it was a lie, but too damn proud to admit it. "You force me night after night. If I'm exhausted it's because of you..."

To her surprise, Ryder laughed at her. She knew she was being unreasonable and ridiculous, but he'd made her so angry and lashing out at him helped ease her frustration. But when he found her words humorous, that infuriated her all the more.

"You're lying to yourself if you believe that. You want to make love as much as I do, even more."

"No," she cried, shaking her head wildly.

"Oh, yes, you do."

He kissed her then, his lips moist and seductive. His tongue slipped inside her mouth with sinful expertise and although she tensed and tried to resist him she soon discovered that it was a mistake to even try to free herself. Her efforts to escape forced the rock-hard contour of his body familiarly close to hers. Her traitorous body sprang to life, responding to him the way a child does to praise. Soon her gasps of anger became tiny moans of pleasure.

"Stop it, Ryder," she cried when he broke off the kiss, pushing at him, wanting out of his arms before she begged him to make love to her.

"Why?"

"I don't like it."

"Oh, but you do," he returned with supreme arrogance; his eyes continued to laugh at her. "Do you really want me to show you how much you like it?"

"No." She pushed again at his shoulders once more.

He cupped her breast in his hand and to her horror, her nipples rose, eager to meet the lazy caress of his fingers. The center of her breasts beaded so hard that even the double layer of material of her exercise outfit couldn't disguise her arousal. Within seconds every part of her was throbbing.

Lynn swallowed a weak groan and sank her teeth into her bottom lip when Ryder caught her earlobe between his lips and tugged on it. "I don't suppose you like this, either?"

"No." Her hands fell lifelessly to her sides. Even a token protest was more than she could muster.

"I thought not," he returned in a husky murmur. "Or this, either." He positioned his hips, presenting his masculinity to her in the rawest form, rubbing against her, teasing her, taunting her with his arousal.

Lynn was convinced it was a miracle she didn't sink to the floor. Every fiber of her being was alive and singing, demanding the release he'd made so remarkably familiar to her.

He slipped his hand from her proud breast to her thigh, in between her long legs, searching higher and higher until Lynn wanted to rip off her clothes.

"Want me, baby?"

She nodded, her whole body weak with longing.

He rewarded her with a kiss that liquified anything that was left of her defenses.

"That's too bad," he whispered, his own voice shaking. She opened her eyes slowly and discovered him staring at her, his gaze clouded with passion. "I want you, too, but you need your rest."

It took a moment for his words to sink in to her consciousness and when they did, she wanted to die. Lynn felt as if she'd suffered a blow to her midsection. Feeling sick to her stomach, she scooted past him and brushed the hair from her flushed face. With deliberate movements, she picked up the bacon off the floor, her hands shaking so badly it was a wonder she could manage that.

Ryder slowly moved away from her. "I'll go get us something for dinner," he told her in a voice that was filled with strain. "Take a hot bath and go to bed. You're exhausted—I'll take care of everything here."

"You don't need to do that, Ryder. I'll fix dinner."

His answering sigh was filled with defeat. "Do what you want, then."

The sound of the front door closing sounded like thunder. Lynn stretched out her hand and grabbed hold of the counter, needing it to remain upright.

"Can we come down now?" Jason called from the top of the stairs.

"Sure." It took effort to keep her voice from pitching and wobbling.

"Where'd Ryder go?" Michelle wanted to know when she joined her mother in the kitchen. She looked around suspiciously as though she expected to find him hiding under the table.

"He...he's going to bring us back something to eat."

"I wish he'd taken me with him," Jason said, whining just a little. "We haven't had hamburgers in a long time and I was hoping for a little variety."

"Ryder didn't need to leave," Michelle pointed out. "He could've ordered pizza. We haven't had that in a while either—not like we used to when you first came back from Hawaii. What's he bringing us?"

"I don't know." Lynn turned back to the sink, not wanting her children to know how close she was to bursting into tears.

"I thought you guys were going to have a big fight," Michelle said, "We listened, but we didn't even hear you shout."

"We...didn't. I think I'll go up and take a shower if you two don't need me."

"Sure, Mom, go ahead."

She raced up the stairs, undressed and turned on the water spigots. Tears scalded her cheeks as she heaved in giant gulps of oxygen. The water didn't ease any of the ache she was experiencing, but then she'd known it wouldn't. When she was finished, she dressed in her pajamas and stood at the top of the stairs.

"Michelle, would you tell Ryder when he gets back that I'm tired and I've decided to go to bed?"

"Okay," she answered with some reluctance.

"But, Mom, it's not even seven," Jason objected.

"I'm really exhausted tonight," she said and turned away to swallow a sob. "He'll understand."

Since that was exactly where he'd sent her, she doubted that Ryder would object. Although she listened for him, Ryder didn't come upstairs until several hours later. Lynn had snoozed off and on for most of the evening, but she was instantly awake the minute

Ryder entered the bedroom. The illuminated dial on the clock radio revealed it was after eleven.

He didn't turn on the light, but she heard him undressing in the dark, taking pains to be quiet.

"I'm awake," she whispered. "Do you want to talk?"

"Not particularly."

If her mood had improved, his hadn't. Sullen silence filled the room.

"I'll stop on my way home tomorrow night and buy groceries," she offered a couple of minutes later, regretting the things she'd said and done and looking for a way to show him how sorry she was.

"While I was out earlier, I picked up a few essentials, so there's no rush." Ryder lifted the sheets and climbed into the bed, staying as far away from her as space would allow.

"I promise I'll do it tomorrow."

"Before or after you put in a ten-hour day?"

Lynn let that comment slide. "It's this membership campaign. You know it won't be like this every week, I promise. By the end of the month things will have settled back to normal."

He bunched up the pillow and rolled onto his side, presenting her with a clear view of his back.

More tortuous seconds passed.

"I'm sorry for the things I said earlier—none of them were true." She tried again, feeling more wretched by the minute, desperate to repair the damage her pride had inflicted.

He didn't respond and she felt a growing desolation. "Ryder, I love you so much, please don't do this . . . I can't bear it."

She felt him stiffen as though a battle were raging within him. It seemed like an eternity passed before he shifted his weight and turned onto his back. Lynn eagerly scooted into his arms, looping her arm around his waist and burying her face between his shoulder and his neck. It felt like coming home after being away a long while, his arms a shelter from the worst storms. Only this hurricane had been one of her own making.

"You can't go on like this," he whispered into her hair, tenderly brushing it away from her face. "I refuse to let you do this to yourself, to your family."

She could only agree. "I've been doing a lot of thinking, between catnaps tonight," she admitted. "I think I understand what's been happening with Slender, Too, the last few months, and why I've pushed myself the way I have."

"You do?"

Lynn nodded. "The first couple of years after Gary was gone, I floundered terribly. Everything in my life was dictated by other people while I struggled for some kind of control. Bit by bit, I gained my independence in small ways. When I was ready to really break free and soar on my own, I bought the franchise. It was the first time in my life that I'd invested in something that was completely mine. I was the one in charge. Slender, Too, was a tiny piece of life that I could govern and the success or failure rested entirely on my shoulders. That first sample of accomplishment was powerful and the taste of independence addictive. I've clung on to it, refusing to let go of even the most mundane aspects of the business, despite the fact that the children didn't have as much attention as they'd wanted. I needed the time for *me*."

"But you're willing to now?"

"Yes, I have to, because I've learned how important my family is in my life. And..."

"Yes?"

"You did that, Ryder."

Then he kissed her until her heart was pounding out of control. "Ah, Lynn, you know exactly what to say to turn my head."

She giggled, loving the feel of his hands as they sought her breasts, rolling her nipples between his supple fingers.

"I want to change things, Ryder, but I'm not sure I know how."

"What you need is a manager to take some of the responsibility off your shoulders."

"But I still want to maintain some control," she inserted, knowing the role of observer would never satisfy her.

"You will have, honey, just not all the hours. Try it out and see how it works."

She nodded, knowing he was right, but still having trouble admitting it—she always *did* have problems owning up to that.

He closed his arms more securely around her. "About what happened in the kitchen," he murmured, flicking his tongue over her ear, nibbling on her lobe.

"Yes?"

Ryder's hand lifted her breast. "Don't you think it's time we finished what we started?"

Eighteen

"Ryder," Lynn purred, utterly content. She slid her bare leg seductively down his much longer one and toyed with the soft hairs at his nape. She was resting on her back and he was lying on his stomach with his hand draped over her middle. "I love you."

"Hmm ... I know." He raised himself up on one elbow and kissed her in a leisurely exercise. "But if anyone should complain about being kept awake nights, it's me."

"Very funny." She rubbed her hands over his back, pausing at the dip below his waist, then hesitated. "I want to talk to you about something important."

He caught her lower lip between his teeth and sucked gently. "What?"

"Gary."

Ryder went completely still. She felt his breath lodge in his throat and his body tense. "Why?"

"Because every time I mention his name, you freeze up and change the subject."

His mouth descended over hers while he rooted through her long hair as though to punish her for bringing Gary's name into their conversation. Lynn gave a painful yelp and he relaxed his grip and lifted his head. His lungs made a soft rustling sound. "That's because I don't want to talk about him."

She smiled gently, and whispered, "I guessed as much, but, Ryder, I don't think that's healthy." Except for their initial discussion at the picnic, from the time he'd returned from Boston, Ryder had gone to great lengths to avoid talking about his best friend.

Again and again he'd assured Lynn that his love for her had nothing to do with what had happened to Gary or any guilt associated with the tragedy of his death. Perhaps because she'd wanted to believe it so badly, she'd held on to the assumption. But lately little things had started to add up and she didn't like the sum total she was seeing. Tonight seemed to be the one to settle their qualms. This problem with Gary was important and she wanted to lay it to rest.

"He's dead, Lynn."

"But that shouldn't mean—"

"You're my wife now."

"I'm not contesting that."

"It's a damn good thing." He tried the playful approach in an effort to beset her, planting kisses on the edges of her mouth, then darting his tongue in and out in a teasing game that would have easily turned her mind an hour earlier.

"Ryder, please," she begged.

He emitted a low guttural sound and chuckled. "I love it when you say that."

"You're impossible!"

He slipped his hand from her breast to her stomach and the amusement drained from his eyes.

Emotion flickered through them, his expression roguish and sexy. Lynn sucked in her breath as he threatened to slide his fingers farther down to the junction between her legs. She quickly stopped him before he could turn the course of their conversation. "You're doing it again."

"I plan to do it every day of our married life."

"Ryder..."

"I want a baby," he announced without warning. "I know we agreed to wait, but I need to get you pregnant now. Tonight. Right now. I can't wait a minute more to feel my son moving inside you."

The plea that came into his voice was almost desperate. "I've thought about it a good deal this past month. Living with Michelle and Jason has taught me so much," he continued, holding her gaze. "I often wondered what kind of a father I'd be. I've even worried about it, but now I know I'm going to love having children."

"Oh, Ryder." She was eager, too, but a little afraid.

His finger cupped the underside of her breast, lifting it, worshiping it. "I want to watch our child suckle your breast and if you'll let me," he paused and his voice dipped. "I'd like to taste your milk." He kissed her nipple with a reverence, flicking his tongue over the rosy peak.

She nodded, unable to refuse him anything.

His face, poised above her own, filled with wonder. His jaw was clenched tight, but not with anger—some other emotion, restraint, she decided. His eyes shone with more vulnerability than she had ever seen in him. Just gazing up at this man she had married, and her heart felt as if it would burst.

"I remember how you had morning sickness with Michelle and Jason. I only want one baby...just one," he said, and laid his hand against her cheek, rubbing his thumb over her lower lip. "But promise me you'll throw out those damn birth control pills."

Tears gathered in the corners of her eyes as she nodded. "Ryder, I love you. I'll give you a dozen children
if that's what you want."

"Dear God, Lynn, will I ever get enough of you?"

"I sincerely hope not." She twisted around, so that
she was on her stomach, and reached for the knot behind her head that would unravel the long plait of hair.
Ryder watched her movements with wide-eyed wonder,
as though he couldn't believe what she was preparing to
do. Obediently he rolled onto his back when her fingers directed him there.

"Lynn."

She rose to a kneeling position, and dragged her hair
across his chest in a light dusting motion, meant to tan-
talize and tease.

He made a grunting sound and caught the long dark
strands with his hands as it swirled around his manhood. She leaned forward and pressed a moist kiss over
the firm muscles of his stomach, taking tiny love bites
that faintly nipped his tender skin.

With a hand on either side of her waist, Ryder lifted
her atop him. Acting purely on instinct, Lynn secured
her hips and carefully lowered herself onto him.

Ryder moaned and his hands bit into the rounded
part of her hips. "Lynn...dear God."

They both paused, taking in huge, calming breaths.
He felt enormous, but her only thought was to draw
him deeper inside her as if the action would make him
a part of her.

"I've never done this before," she admitted breathlessly, watching the play of pleasure as it knit its way
across his tight features. Not knowing what else to do,
she rolled her hips once. "You'll have to show me..."

"Yes, Lynn...yes, do that."

Lynn complied, led by instinct, she closed her eyes and shifted as she had before in a slow, grinding motion, eager to give him the satisfaction he had so often given her.

Ryder reached up and covered her breasts with his hands. If he meant to instruct her further, his words were lost in an avalanche of sexual gratification that dominated them both.

It wasn't until Lynn was dressing the following morning that she discovered Gary's uniform hat and badge were missing. She'd kept them stored on the shelf above the closet in their bedroom, carefully packed away in a box she planned to give Jason when he turned eighteen.

She paused, uncertain. Removing Gary's photo from the living room was one thing, but for Ryder to take away something that was a part of her son's inheritance was another. After a short search, she found Gary's photos and several other items stored in the garage, tucked away in a secluded corner.

Lynn exhaled sharply, remembering how she'd tried to talk to Ryder about Gary just the night before. But Ryder had done it to her again. Now that she gave the matter thought, Lynn realized that Michelle and Jason rarely mentioned their deceased father anymore, either. They, too, had apparently sensed Ryder's uneasiness over the subject and had eliminated Gary's name from casual conversation.

Following that episode with the missing hat and badge, Lynn was more determined than ever to have this out with Ryder. It was paramount that they discuss Gary and the role he now played in their lives. Ryder seemed to want to shove him aside and pretend he'd never existed. The only reason she could figure why he would do something like that wasn't one she was eager to face. If Ryder continued to carry a burden of guilt over Gary's death, then she could never be fully certain of his motive for marrying her and taking on the responsibility of raising Michelle and Jason.

She loved him. The children loved him. Ryder had made certain of that. He'd done everything humanly possible to garner their affection. He spoiled Michelle and Jason, taking his duty as stepfather far beyond what anyone would have expected. In analyzing the situation, Lynn realized it was as if Ryder was trying to make up to them for all the years they'd gone without a father figure.

The knot in her stomach twisted into a tighter knot.

When it came to proving his devotion to her, Ryder had seemed determined to be the model husband. He brought her gifts, made love to her frequently, and spoiled her in much the same way he did the children, as if he needed to compensate her for the loss of Gary.

A week passed, and although Lynn tried twice more to talk about her dead husband, Ryder wouldn't allow it. He was never abrupt or angry in his efforts to avoid the subject, but firmly subtle. She would carefully plan the discussion, wait for a quiet moment, usually after Michelle and Jason were in bed, and fifteen minutes later she would marvel at just how skillful Ryder's methods were of dodging the issue.

The problem was that they were both so busy. Ryder's caseload was increasing, which meant he left for work earlier and arrived home later. On her end, Lynn had offered the job of manager, with an appropriate increase in salary, to her assistant, Sharon. Her employee seemed both pleased and surprised and had eagerly accepted the promotion. That same week, Lynn hired another new assistant and left her training in Sharon's capable hands.

Lynn was still needed at the salon, but much of the day-to-day responsibility fell onto Sharon, which surprisingly pleased Lynn. She thought she would miss the control, but her life was so full that it was a relief not to worry about Slender, Too along with everything else.

On Wednesday, Lynn decided to try once more to talk to Ryder. This time, she wouldn't be put off so easily.

"I'm going to lunch now," Sharon informed Lynn, sticking her head into the office. "Judy's taking the noon class, but this is her first time going solo, so you might want to keep an eye on her."

"Will do," Lynn answered with a smile. She was reviewing the work schedule, penciling in names and times for the following week.

Sharon left the door to the office ajar, and the upbeat melody for the aerobics class drifted into the room. Absently Lynn tapped her foot, but the action stopped abruptly as her eyes fell on the following Monday's date.

It was silly that such a minor thing would trouble her so—Gary's birthday—or what would have been his birthday. He would have been thirty-seven, only Gary would remain thirty-three forever.

The remainder of the day was melancholy. Lynn found herself pensive and blue. She wouldn't change her life from the way it was now—she had no regrets— but a certain sadness permeated her being. One she couldn't shake or fully understand.

She was home before the kids, which was unusual. She left the salon early, telling Sharon she had a headache.

"Mom, I'm going over to Marcy's. Okay?" Michelle asked ten minutes after she was in the door.

"That's fine, honey."

Jason was holding an apple and a banana in one hand and a box of graham crackers in the other. "Do we have any chocolate chip cookies left?" He must have noticed her frown because he added, "I'm a growing boy—I need my afternoon snack."

"Take the apple and a few of the crackers, I don't want you ruining your dinner."

"Oh, Mom."

He may not have agreed, but he willingly obeyed her.

The pork chops were ready for the oven and the house was quiet. The real-estate agent they'd been working with phoned to tell Lynn about a large colonial that had just come on the market.

"Would you like to make an appointment to see it this evening?"

Lynn's gaze scooted around the kitchen and family room, falling lovingly on each wall and each piece of furniture. She didn't want to move, she never had. Ryder had been the one who insisted they start looking for another home right away. The day they returned from their honeymoon, he'd contacted a realtor. At least Lynn had been able to convince him not to put their house on the market until they found something suitable.

"Mrs. Matthews?"

"Not tonight," she answered abruptly, realizing she'd left the woman hanging. "Perhaps tomorrow...I'm not feeling well." Considering her mood, that wasn't so far from the truth.

When she finished with the phone conversation, Lynn sat and covered her face with her hands. In the bottom drawer of the china cabinet was her and Gary's wedding album. She felt drawn to that. Reverently she removed the bulky book and folded back the cover and the first thick page as though turning something fragile. The picture of her and Gary, standing with their wedding party, both so young and so much in love, greeted her like an old friend.

Tears flooded Lynn's eyes. Tears she couldn't fully comprehend.

She loved Ryder . . . she loved Gary.

The front door opened and thinking it was one of the children, Lynn wiped the moisture from her cheek and forced a smile.

Instead Ryder sauntered into the room. It was hours before he was due home. "Did the realtor call to set an appointment for us to see that new house?"

"I . . . I told her we'd look at it another day," she answered abruptly, quickly closing the picture album.

Ryder frowned. "I called the salon, but Sharon told me you'd gone home because of a headache."

Feeling incredibly guilty, Lynn stood abruptly and moved in front of the table. "I'm fine." She rubbed her palms together in an agitated movement and stepped across the room, praying Ryder wouldn't notice the picture album.

Ryder hesitated. "You've been crying."

"Not really . . . something must have gotten into my eye."

"Lynn, what's wrong?"

"Nothing." She moved to the coffeepot and poured herself a cup, although she already had one. When she turned back, she found Ryder standing at the round oak table, his hand on the wedding portfolio. He lifted back the cover.

Watching him, Lynn wanted to cry out for him to stop, but she knew it wouldn't do any good. His narrowed gaze rested on the picture she had been studying. He seemed to stop breathing. She looked on helplessly as he clenched his jaw, but the action wasn't directed by anger. Somehow, she'd expected him to become irate, but the look on his face revealed far more pain than irritation.

"You're still in love with him, aren't you?"

Nineteen

"Yes," Lynn admitted. "I love Gary."

The blood drained from Ryder's face as though she'd physically punched him. After the initial shock, he wore a look that claimed he'd known it all along, and wasn't the least bit surprised.

"Ryder... I was married to the man for nine years. Michelle and Jason are his children. I'm not the kind of woman who can conveniently forget that. Yes, I love Gary and as much as you don't want to hear it, I'm not likely to ever forget him."

"Gary is dead."

"You're making it sound like I'm being unfaithful to you by remembering him. I can't pretend the man never existed and neither can you."

"Thinking about him is one thing, but do you have to moon over his pictures, grieving your terrible loss?"

"His death *was* a terrible loss," she cried, losing patience. "And I wasn't mooning!"

"I find you weeping while looking over pictures of your wedding to another man and you try to feed me some line about there being something in your eye. You don't even have to say it. I can tell you regret the fact we're married."

"I don't. How can you ever think such a thing?"

"You honestly expect me to answer that? How many other times have you taken out that wedding album and cried over Gary?"

"This is the first time . . . in months. I don't even remember the last time I felt like this. He was my husband, I have the right to look at these pictures and feel sad."

"Not when you're married to me."

"I will if I damn well please," she cried defensively.

Ryder's mouth thinned. "I'm your husband, Lynn."

"I know that." His attitude was infuriating her more every minute.

"What possible reason would you have to drag out those old pictures and weep over him now?"

Lynn's hands knotted in defense, knowing Ryder wasn't going to like her answer. "It's his birthday next week."

Ryder took three abrupt steps away from her, halted and jerked his fingers through his hair. "The man is dead. He doesn't have birthdays."

"I'm well aware of that. But I can't forget the fact he lived and breathed and loved."

Ryder began pacing and seemed to mull over her words. "The loving part is the crux of the problem, isn't it?"

"Of course," she cried. "I know that bothers you, and I'm sorry, but I can't change the past anymore than I could raise Gary from the dead. He was an important part of my life and I don't plan on forgetting him because you can't bear the mention of his name."

Ryder went still as if a new thought had flashed into his mind. His dark eyes hardened. "You blame me for his death, too, don't you? I'd always feared you would, and then I chose to overlook the obvious."

"Oh, Ryder, honestly," she whispered, wanting to weep, "I don't blame you. I never did—I couldn't have married you if there'd been doubt in my heart."

He shook his head, discounting her answer. "The revenge would be sweet. If you'd planned to torture me, you couldn't have chosen a more painful method."

"Stop talking like that. It's crazy—I love you. Hasn't the past month taught you that much?"

"I did this to myself," he murmured, defeated. "There's no one else to blame." He inhaled a long, slow breath, and continued thoughtfully. "I rushed you into the marriage, using every trick I could think of, and like a fool, I didn't even consider the fact you planned to hold on to Gary with both hands."

"I'm not holding on to Gary—you're being utterly ridiculous."

"Am I?"

The fight seemed to have died in him, Lynn noticed. He was resolved now, subdued, as if he'd lost the most important battle of his life.

"I honestly thought I could step into Michelle's and Jason's lives and fill the void left by Gary's death. Only there wasn't one. You've carried his image in your heart and on your lips all these years. They didn't need a father, not when the memory of Gary remained so strong. You made sure of that."

"Ryder..."

"You didn't need a husband, either."

"You're right," she cried, her patience gone. "I didn't *need* one, but I *wanted* you..."

"In bed."

"In my life," she cried. Tears of anger and frustration brimmed in her eyes and she wiped them aside, furious that she couldn't hold back the emotion.

His smile was unbelievably sad. "I knew you loved Gary in the beginning, but I thought once we were married that would change."

"Change?"

He ignored her question and walked over to the kitchen window, looking out onto the back patio, although Lynn felt certain he was blind to the glory of the late summer afternoon. "The realtor has taken us to look at how many houses now?"

He was jumping from one subject to another, without any logical reason that she could decipher. "What has that got to do with anything?"

"Ten homes? Fifteen? And yet you've never been able to find one you like. The house may be perfect for us, but you've always managed to come up with a convenient excuse why we shouldn't buy it."

"I—"

"Have you ever considered the reason all those homes didn't suit you? Why you've continued to drag your feet again and again? It's getting to the point now that you delay even setting up the appointment with the realtor."

She wanted to shout at him, tell him how wrong he was, but as far as the realtor went, she was guilty of everything he claimed. "I...oh, Ryder, I never *did* want to move. I'm trying, but there are so many happy memories associated with this place. I love it here, I'm comfortable."

"And I'm not."

She dipped her head and eased her breath out on a disheartened sigh. "I know."

"Gary's ghost is here, in every room, and he's haunted me from the minute we returned from Hawaii. Every time I walk through the front door, I feel his presence, every time I turn around, his face is looking at me, accusing me. I tried to ignore him, tried to pretend he wasn't there. I went so far as to remove his pictures and a few other things, thinking that would help, but it didn't.''

Lynn wasn't sure what to say. She could understand his feelings, although that didn't help their situation any.

"But a new house isn't going to solve that, is it, Lynn?"

"How do you mean?"

"Gary's a part of you in the same way that he's a part of Michelle and Jason. We won't ever be able to escape him, because wherever you are, he'll be there, too."

She opened her mouth to deny that, then realized that, too, was the truth.

"I notice you're not bothering to repudiate that fact."

Lynn drooped her head as the defeat worked its way through her tired limbs. "No, I don't think I can. You're right."

"I thought as much." If he experienced any elation at correctly deciphering her actions, it wasn't evident in his voice. What *did* come through was a heavy note of despair. "I can't continue to fool myself any longer and neither can you. Nothing's going to change."

"I don't understand why it should," she cried. "You're asking me to wipe out a decade of my life, and I find that unreasonable. It's just not going to happen."

"You don't need to tell me that, I figured it out already." He reached out and touched her, lightly grazing her cheek with his fingertips, his eyes filled with an agony of regret. "I won't take second place in your life, Lynn."

The action tugged at Lynn's heart and she caught his hand in her own, wanting to weep and beg him to understand. She managed to hold all the emotion boiling within her at bay; she longed to find the words that would reassure him, but was at a loss.

"I love you, Ryder."

He nodded, sadly. "But not enough."

With that he turned and slowly climbed the stairs.

Lynn followed him a couple of minutes later and was shocked to see him packing his suitcases.

"What are you doing?"

"Giving us both some needed space to think things out."

"But you're moving out. Why?" Tears gushed down her face—she didn't even try to hold them inside.

"I was wrong to have married you," Ryder said, busily filling his luggage, hardly stopping to look at her.

"Well, that's just wonderful," she cried and slumped onto the edge of the mattress. Her legs felt incredibly weak. "So you're going to walk out on me. It's getting to be a habit with you, Ryder. A bad habit. When the going gets tough, the tough move on, is that it? Where are you going this time? Europe? Do you think that'll be far enough away to forget?"

He whirled around. "You've already admitted you still love Gary, what else do you expect me to do?"

"I also admitted that I love *you*! Love me back, accept me for who I am—love Michelle and Jason. I want you to give me the child you've talked about so much, and build a good life with me and our children."

"And play second fiddle to a dead man? No thanks." He slammed the lid closed on the first suitcase and reached for the second.

"Why are you doing this?" she cried.

He hesitated. "You already know the answer to that. There isn't any need to discuss it further."

Desperate now, Lynn scooted off the bed and walked over to the window. She closed her eyes and covered her mouth with her hand. "Aren't I even allowed to keep the memories?"

He didn't respond, which was answer enough.

"Can't I?" she tried again, tears drenching her face, dripping onto her chin. She brushed them off with the heel of her hand, and held her head high, the action dictated by an abundance of pride.

"Go ahead and leave me, Ryder. Walk out on me. I got along without you the first time, I'll do it again." She marched across the room to the closet and ripped his dress shirts off the hangers one by one in a disorderly fashion. "I wouldn't want you to forget anything," she sobbed. "Take it all."

He carelessly stuffed the pressed shirts in the bottom of the garment bag, paused and glance around. "I'll send someone for whatever else is left."

"Fine." She didn't dare look at him, for fear she would break down completely and beg him to stay. "Just be sure this is what you really want."

He hesitated, his gaze mirroring her own agony. "It isn't, but I think a separation will give us both time to sort through our feelings."

"How long? One year? Three? Or should we try to break a record this time?"

Ryder closed his eyes, as though her words were a physical assault. Lynn frantically wiped the moisture from her face. "I tried to talk to you about Gary," she sobbed. "God knows, I tried, but you'd never let me. The minute I mentioned his name you did cartwheels in an effort to change the subject."

"The reason should have been obvious."

"If we'd been able to clear the air before...then maybe none of this would be necessary. But oh no, you insisted on sweeping everything under the carpet—ignore it and it'll go away. But Gary isn't going and neither am I!"

"I didn't want to hear what you were so bound and determined to tell me," he shouted. "In this instance, ignorance was bliss." He swung the suitcases off the mattress with such force it tugged the bedspread onto the floor.

Lynn righted it as though that was of the utmost importance.

Ryder left the bedroom, walking away from her with ground-devouring steps, as if he couldn't get away fast enough. Lynn remained in the bedroom, and flinched at the sound of the front door closing as it echoed up the stairway.

The silence that followed was as profound as it was deafening.

Lynn didn't know how long she stood there, immobile and numb. The floor seemed to sway and buckle under her feet and she lowered herself onto the edge of the bed, her fingers biting into the mattress.

The tears had dried against the flushed skin of her cheeks long before she was composed enough to go downstairs and confront Michelle and Jason.

"When's dinner?" Jason asked as he barged in the front door a few minutes later with Michelle close behind him.

"I'm...just putting it on now." She quietly put the pork chops into the oven, all the time knowing she wouldn't be able to gag down a single bite of the evening meal.

"You haven't even started yet?"

"It's only five," Michelle said indignantly.

"I need something to carry me through," Jason cried. He opened the cookie jar and stuck in his hand. The bowl had been empty all week, but her son managed to gain a pawful of crumbs and took delight in licking them from his hand a finger at a time as he walked out of the kitchen.

"I don't suppose you thought to wash your hands before you did that?" Michelle commented, having gone to position herself in front of the television. "Aren't you going to tell him to wash, Mom? He could be bringing in germs that will infect us all."

"It would be like closing the gate after the horse gets loose," she said, doing her best to pretend everything was normal.

"When's Ryder getting home?" Jason asked, opening the refrigerator and peering inside.

"He's...going to be away on a business trip for a while," she said as nonchalantly as possible, trying to play down the fact he was missing without arousing their suspicions.

The door to the refrigerator closed with a bang. "When did he tell you this?"

She glanced at the clock. "An hour ago."

"How long is he going to be gone?" Jason asked anxiously. "What about soccer? What am I going to tell the coach when Ryder doesn't show up...I'm counting on him and so is everyone else. I play better when Ryder's there watching me."

"I...don't know what you should tell Mr. Lawson...tell him Ryder had to go out of town."

"He could have said something to us, don't you think?" Michelle said with a pout. "I need him to help me with my math. We're dividing fractions and some of those problems are too hard for me and a simple calculator. I've got to have massive help."

"You can do it, Michelle, I'll be around to lend a hand."

"Thanks, but no thanks," she said, on a sarcastic note. "I remember the last time you decided to tutor me in fractions. I'm lucky I made it out of fifth grade."

"Why would Ryder leave on a business trip?" Jason wanted to know, his eyes curious. "I thought all his cases were in Seattle."

Lynn hated to lie to her children, but she didn't want to alarm them unnecessarily. She would tell them the truth, but not now when it was difficult enough for her to face.

The dinner was one of the best Lynn had fixed all week, but no one seemed to have much of an appetite.

"Ryder's coming back, isn't he, Mom?" Michelle whispered the question while Lynn removed their plates from the table. Jason was talking to Brad on the telephone.

"Of course he is," she returned with an encouraging grin that took all her reserve of strength. She didn't know what had prompted the question and prayed her daughter didn't notice the way her hands shook as she placed their dinner dishes in the dishwasher.

Michelle relaxed. "It's been good having a dad again."

"I know." It had been good having a husband, too. But Lynn had the crippling feeling that this problem with Ryder wasn't going to be settled overnight.

"Ryder's going to phone us, isn't he?" Jason asked, once he was finished talking to his friend. "Brad's father goes on business trips sometimes and he calls every night. Brad says it's really great because when his dad comes home, he brings him and his little sister gifts."

"I don't know if Ryder will have a chance to call," Lynn said, making busywork around the sink, scrubbing it extra hard. Her eyes blurred with fresh tears.

"He'll bring us back a present, won't he?"

"I . . . don't know that, either."

Jason uttered a disgruntled sound. "What's the use of having him go away, if he doesn't bring us back something?"

"Maybe he doesn't know he's supposed to," Michelle murmured thoughtfully. "He didn't have any kids until us. Maybe we should all write him and drop the hint. I'm sure he'd want to know what his duties are to me and Jason."

Lynn couldn't endure another minute of their exchange. Ryder claimed Gary's ghost filled their house and that their children held on to his memory. If Ryder were there to hear this conversation now, he would know how untrue that was.

The evening seemed to drag. Although Michelle claimed she didn't want Lynn's help with her math, after several minutes of grumbling over her assignment, she succumbed and took everything to her mother. When Lynn wasn't much help, Michelle suggested they call Lynn's accountant.

As expected, Jason put up a fuss about taking a bath, but that was normal. Lynn's patience was stretched to its limit. Jason must have known that because after voicing the usual arguments, he went upstairs and bathed in world-record time. Lynn wondered if he'd managed to get his entire body wet, but hadn't the fight in her to question him.

The kids were in their rooms when the front door opened.

"Ryder," Jason cried from the top of the stairs, racing into his arms. "What happened on your business trip? Did you know when you go away you're supposed to bring back presents for your kids? It's the expected thing.''

"You're not supposed to blurt it out like that!" Michelle stormed. "You can be such a nerd, sometimes."

"Who's calling who a nerd?"

"Children, please," Lynn cried moving into the entryway. She sought Ryder's gaze, but he avoided meeting hers.

"How come you're home?" Michelle asked. "You haven't even been gone a single night."

"The plane was late," Ryder told her. He glanced at his watch. "Now go back upstairs, it's long past your bed time."

"Okay."

"Do we have to?"

"Yes, you do," Lynn answered for Ryder. "Good night to you both."

"You missed a great dinner," Jason added, hugging him one last time. "Mom cooked her special pork chops."

If pork chops would have kept Ryder home, Lynn would cook them every night.

"I'll see you in the morning," Jason said on the tail end of a yawn. "I hope you stay home...it's not right when you're gone."

Both Michelle and Jason had returned to their bedrooms before Ryder spoke. "I apologize for dropping in like this, but I forgot my briefcase. There are some papers I'll need in the morning, otherwise I wouldn't have troubled you."

Twenty

Ryder scooted past Lynn and retrieved his briefcase. Lynn stood frozen, her heart jackhammering against her rib cage, but she dared not move for fear she would break down and weep before he left.

Ryder returned, and paused in front of the door. "I take it you told the kids I was going away on a business trip?"

She nodded. "I probably shouldn't have lied, but I didn't know what else to say."

"That explanation is as good as any. Once they get used to the idea of me being gone, you can tell them the truth."

"Which is?"

"Which is," he repeated and drew in an unsteady breath, "I needed to get away for a while...to think things through."

"I'm sure they'll understand that readily enough." Her voice dipped sarcastically. "And what should I tell them you're thinking about? They'll ask me that, you know. Exactly what do you want me to tell them?"

"You know the answer to that," he snapped.

"I don't."

"I'm trying to decide if I can continue to live with a woman who's in love with another man."

Lynn crossed her arms over her middle to ward off a chill that descended over her like an October frost. "You make it sound so vile, as though I'm committing adultery by honoring Gary's memory."

"You do more than honor his memory, despite what we have, you won't let him go."

"No..." Her voice cracked, and she whirled around, unable to face him any longer. "I love you, Ryder, and it's going to break my heart to lose you, but I don't know what I can do to make things right for us."

He was silent for so long, Lynn wondered if he'd slipped out the door without her hearing him move, but she didn't turn around to investigate.

Suddenly the tension of the day overwhelmed her. Tears flooded her eyes and she sobbed so hard her shoulders shook violently.

A bedroom door opened upstairs. "Mom?"

"It's all right, Jason," Ryder answered.

"I can hear Mom crying." Her son started down the stairs, pausing halfway down. "She *is* crying."

Lynn wiped the moisture from her face as best she could. "I'm fine, honey."

"Ryder," Jason shouted. "Do something...hold her or kiss her or do that other stuff women like. You can't let her stand there like that, bawling her head off."

Ryder hesitated, then walked over to Lynn's side. He didn't want to touch her, she could feel his reluctance, but they both knew Jason wouldn't be appeased until he was assured his mother was receiving the comfort she needed. Ryder wrapped his arms around her and Lynn buried her face in his shoulder, her arms hanging limply at her sides.

"You've got to hold on to him, too, Mom," Jason instructed impatiently.

Lynn complied, awkwardly. Her raised arms loosely circled Ryder's waist. Being this close to him demanded a steep fee and she quivered, wondering how she would ever adjust to a life where there wouldn't be someone to love her the way Ryder did. Her whole body felt as if it were trembling from the inside out.

"I don't think you should be taking this business trip," Jason announced, marching the rest of the way down the stairs, with a military crispness that would have pleased the Green Berets.

Lynn backed out of Ryder's arms and made an effort to compose herself. "Honey, listen—"

"Ryder didn't say anything about going away on business trips when he married us."

"I'm sorry, son, but I have to leave." Ryder's own voice was dark and heavy.

"But we need you here. Mom tried not to show it, but Michelle and I noticed how miserable she was all night. She misses you a whole bunch already and you've only been gone a little while."

Ryder's gaze fell on Lynn and a weary sadness invaded his eyes.

"Michelle and I need you, too. Mom had to help Michelle with her math tonight and it didn't go very well."

"I'm sure your mother did just fine."

"Not according to Michelle," Jason murmured, tossing Lynn an apologetic glance. "I don't think Mom's into fractions."

"What are you guys talking about down there?" Michelle shouted testily. "I thought we were supposed to be in bed, asleep."

"Mom's crying," Jason shot back at his sister.

"I knew something like this was going to happen,"
Michelle blurted out and raced down the stairs like an
avenging angel of mercy. "I hope you know this is all
your fault, Ryder."

"Michelle," Lynn warned.

"Mom's been a basket case all night. How can you
leave the woman who loves you alone like this?"

So much for the gallant effort she'd made to hide her
distress from the kids. Knowing how woefully she'd
failed, Lynn's lower lip quivered and she was forced to
take in several deep breaths to hold back a fresh batch
of tears. "Michelle and Jason, it's time for you to go
back upstairs."

"Are you going to cry again?" Jason wanted reassurance before he returned to his bedroom.

Lynn shook her head, then realized she couldn't make
that guarantee. "I'll try not to."

Michelle and Jason shared a meaningful glance and
then by unspoken agreement, headed toward their bedrooms. Lynn stopped them at the foot of the stairs,
hugging them separately, loving her children so much
her heart felt as if it would burst with the weight of the
emotion. Gary had given her these precious two and if
there had been no other grounds than that, she would
always love him. As it was there were so many reasons
to love and remember Gary Danfort.

"You want a hug, too, Ryder?" Michelle asked,
yawning out the question with her hand in front of her
face.

He nodded, holding Michelle close. Lynn noted the
way his eyes closed and his jaw tightened.

"Next time when you need to go away," Michelle
murmured, "do try to tell us sooner so we won't all feel
so lonely without you. It's bad when you leave and we

haven't had time to..." she paused, and dragged a huge breath through her lungs, "...prepare for it."

"You're not still going, are you?" Jason cried, shocked. "After all this?"

"Jason, to bed!" Lynn pointed up the stairs, her voice more solid.

"He made you cry and Michelle could flunk math, and Ryder is still going to catch that stupid plane, anyway? Doesn't he know he's got responsibilities...like taking out the garbage and helping coach soccer—"

"We're going to be just fine without Ryder," Lynn interrupted her son's outburst, but her voice lacked any real conviction.

"No, we won't!" Jason proclaimed under his breath. He paused and his eyes flashed with concern. "You'll be back in time for Saturday's game, won't you?"

"I'm not sure."

With that, Jason tossed his arms into the air. "What's the use of having a new dad if he can't come to my soccer games?"

"Jason!"

He muttered something unintelligible under his breath and vanished inside his bedroom.

Lynn straightened her shoulders and tried to offer Ryder a smile to make up for the disruption, but her mouth wouldn't cooperate. It was unlikely that Ryder even noticed since his gaze was centered on the empty hallway upstairs, from where both children had disappeared.

"They love you," Lynn told him softly, wondering if he fully understood how much.

Ryder nodded and reluctantly reached for his briefcase.

Lynn closed her eyes, unable to bear the pain of his leaving. It had been difficult enough the first time. The words to ask him to stay burned on the tip of her tongue, but she was forced to swallow them. The taste of acid filled her dry mouth.

Ryder hesitated in front of the door and then turned back to her. "I don't know that I can do it." Each word seemed to be painfully pulled from his heart, his voice strained and low.

Lynn bowed her head. "I don't know that I can let you."

"By all rights, you should throw me out of here, but I'd like to try to sort this out if we can. Let's talk."

Lynn felt her body go weak with relief, and led the way into the kitchen. She automatically put on a pot of coffee. Ryder stepped behind her, his hands resting lightly on her shoulders as if he needed to touch her.

"I didn't really need the briefcase," he admitted, "I was looking for a convenient excuse to come back and make things right, although God knows, I can't see any solution to this."

Lynn sucked part of her bottom lip with her teeth. It had cost Ryder a good deal of pride to be so honest and she was grateful.

When the coffee had finished dripping into the glass pot, she poured them each a mug and carried them to the table, where Ryder was waiting. She sat across from him.

Ryder cupped his hands around the steaming mug, his eyes downcast. "After what just happened with Michelle and Jason, I realize what a jealous fool I'm being. How can I feel resentful toward a man I loved ... a man who's been dead for over three years?"

"But, Ryder you don't have any reason to be jealous of Gary."

Ryder looked away from her, refusing to meet her eyes. "Please let me finish, Lynn. It's not a pleasant emotion to have to admit to myself, let alone confess to you. I realized while I was driving around tonight that undiluted, hard-core jealousy was exactly what I was feeling."

"But, Ryder, I love you so much."

"I know that, too, but as damning as it sounds, I begrudge every minute of the life you shared with Gary." He stopped and ran his hand over his jaw as if the action would erase the guilt charted across the tight lines of his face. "Admitting it to you this way makes me feel like I've got to be the pettiest man alive. How can I even think like this? What kind of man am I to feel these things? I look around me and this crushing weight of shame is pressed upon me. I loved Gary—he was the best kind of police officer and human being I'm ever likely to know. He was everything that was good . . . honorable and generous . . . he was my friend and yet I'm harboring all these negative emotions toward him."

Lynn reached for Ryder's hand, intertwining their fingers. "You love Gary and you resent Gary . . . it isn't any wonder you haven't wanted to talk about him."

"If he hadn't died, I wouldn't have you and the kids and so there's an incredible amount of guilt involved as well." He sucked in a sigh and slowly shook his head as though the magnitude of his emotions was more than he could fully comprehend. "I honestly believed I'd dealt with all my feelings for him while I was in law school, but I can see now that you were right. I was sweeping all these painful emotions under a carpet, avoiding confronting them because I've been so confused. Hell, I'm still confused." The rugged lines in his face were testament enough to the turmoil churning inside his soul. "I packed my bags and was running away from you and the kids...that was so stupid, so illogical, I can't believe the thought so much as entered my mind. The only place in the world I want to be is with you and Michelle and Jason. My heart is here...my soul is here...there's no leaving, no running away."

Tears bled down the side of Lynn's face. Unable to maintain this distance from her husband any longer, she stood and walked around the table. Ryder scooted out his chair and lowered her into his lap, folding her in his embrace, sighing as her arms circled him.

"I've been doing some thinking tonight myself," Lynn told him, her throat thick with emotion. "And like you, I realize I've made a lot of mistakes. Looking over those wedding pictures was one of them...I can understand how you must have felt when you found me."

"Deep down inside, I know how completely unreasonable I'm being to ask you to forget Gary, but I can't seem to put that behind me."

"Can you forget him?" she asked quietly, cupping his face in her hands.

Ryder's mouth twisted with the question and Lynn could feel the tension in his taut body. "No," he admitted with a strangled breath. "And I'm not sure I want to."

"I can't either. You loved him. I loved him. Michelle and Jason loved him. We can't conveniently forget he lived and touched our lives. We can't pretend a part of him won't always be with us. You love Michelle and

Jason—you have from the time they were born—they're a part of Gary, too.''

"I know . . . I know." But that insight didn't seem to ease Ryder's distress. "Maybe we're going about this all wrong."

Lynn frowned. "How do you mean?"

His arms circled her waist and he pressed his forehead against her shoulder. "For the past few months, I've done everything I could to cast him from our lives. I've resented his intrusion into what I consider my family, but I've been wrong, because you and the kids are his family, too."

"Yes," she answered, not sure she was following his line of reasoning.

"I've tried everything within my power to make everyone forget him. You didn't. Michelle and Jason didn't. And neither did I."

Lynn nodded.

"I can't ignore him any longer, Lynn. If he were here now, we could sit down and talk this out. Man to man."

"But he isn't here."

For the first time that evening, Ryder smiled. "I think he is . . . not in any ghostly form or anything like that, but his spirit is here, his essence. He's a large part of Michelle and Jason . . . and a part of you."

"If Gary were here," she murmured, "and you could talk to him, what would you say?"

Ryder frowned thoughtfully. "I'm not sure. One thing I'd do is tell him how much I love you and explain that I know he felt the same deep commitment to you. I think he'd understand and approve of me marrying you." Some of the weary tautness left his limbs as soon as he'd voiced the thought.

"If Gary had handpicked the man to take his place in our lives, it would have been you."

Ryder relaxed even more with that. "I'd tell him how proud he'd be of his children, and of you," he paused to kiss her lightly.

Some of the strain eased from his eyes and Lynn leaned forward enough to plant a simple kiss on his lips. She ran her fingers through his hair, toying with it because she needed to keep touching and feeling him. "You know what we're doing, don't you?"

Ryder's responding glance confirmed that he didn't.

"We're inviting Gary's memory back into our lives, because excluding him would be futile."

"And wrong," Ryder added in a voice that trembled slightly.

They stared at each other, both sets of eyes glistening with unshed tears. Words weren't necessary now, they would have been superfluous at that moment. Lynn and Ryder had emptied their hearts of any emotion except the gift Gary Danfort had given them—each other.

Lynn wrapped her arms around Ryder's neck and hugged him close, cradling his head against her breast. "Don't you think it's time to unpack those bags?"

He was too busy toying with the front of her blouse. "I think it's time for other things, too."

"Sleep?"

"If you think you're going upstairs to rest, think again, woman."

Slowly their mouths merged, and when they kissed their hearts were open, free from the chains of the past, free to soar in their love.

From National Bestselling Author

DEBBIE MACOMBER

Comes a poignant story of an undeniable attraction

Fallen Angel

Amy Johnson was being groomed to take over her father's company. No one seemed to notice that her heart wasn't in it, that she was miserable. Until a handsome stranger gave her some much-needed advice and a shoulder to lean on. But just when his tempting kisses made Amy hungry for more, Josh Powell was sent to the other side of the world. He left without making any promises or commitments to her.

When circumstances bring them together again, Josh must decide whether he'll let this alluring woman into his life or if he'll let her slip away....

Fall in love with *Fallen Angel,* this October at your favorite retail outlet.

Take 3 of
"The Best of the Best™"
Novels FREE
Plus get a FREE surprise gift!

Special Limited-time Offer

Mail to The Best of the Best™

> 3010 Walden Avenue
> P.O. Box 1867
> Buffalo, N.Y. 14269-1867

YES! Please send me 3 free novels and my free surprise gift. Then send me 3 of "The Best of the Best™" novels each month. I'll receive the best books by the world's hottest romance authors. Bill me at the low price of $3.99 each plus 25¢ delivery and applicable sales tax, if any.* That's the complete price and a savings of over 20% off the cover prices—quite a bargain! I understand that accepting the books and gift places me under no obligation ever to buy any books. I can always return a shipment and cancel at any time. Even if I never buy another book from Harlequin, the 3 free books and the surprise gift are mine to keep forever.

183 BPA A2P5

Name	(PLEASE PRINT)	
Address	Apt. No.	
City	State	Zip

This offer is limited to one order per household and not valid to current subscribers.
*Terms and prices are subject to change without notice. Sales tax applicable in N.Y.
All orders subject to approval.

UBOB-296

©1990 Harlequin Enterprises Limited